"Moved on!" Erith exclaimed

Any attempt to remain cool suddenly shattered. "Then I'll just have to return home."

"Why?" Domengo rapped back, aggressively. "You have some man you can't wait to get back to in England?"

"No, I haven't!" Erith denied hotly when she'd recovered from his astonishing statement.

"Yes, you have!" He refused to let the subject drop. "From the moment you arrived, you've been panting to get back to your lover!"

"Lover!" she snapped in explosive fury. "Don't talk rot! I haven't got a lover. I've never had a lover! And for your information—"

"You've never had a lover?" he challenged fiercely, the look of disbelief on his face telling her all she needed to know....

Jessica Steele first tried her hand at writing romance novels at her husband's encouragement two years after they were married. She fondly remembers the day her first novel was accepted for publication. ''Peter mopped me up, and neither of us cooked that night,'' she recalls. ''We went out to dinner.'' She and her husband live in a hundred-year-old cottage in Worcestershire, and they've traveled to many fascinating places—including China, Japan, Mexico and Denmark—that make wonderful settings for her books.

Books by Jessica Steele

HARLEQUIN ROMANCE

HARLEQUIN PRESENTS

WITHOUT KNOWING WHY

Jessica Steele

Harlequin Books

TORONTO • NEW YORK • LONDON
AMSTERDAM • PARIS • SYDNEY • HAMBURG
STOCKHOLM • ATHENS • TOKYO • MILAN

Original hardcover edition published in 1991
by Mills & Boon Limited

ISBN 0-373-03173-4

Harlequin Romance first edition January 1992

WITHOUT KNOWING WHY

CHAPTER ONE

HERE she was in Cuzco, the capital of the ancient Inca empire, but any excitement that had stirred in Erith at being there had now deserted her.

She had arrived in Peru last night after a journey that had involved landing first in Germany and then in Venezuela. She couldn't have said that 'excitement' had been her chief emotion on that flight—in all honesty she had been more anxious about what awaited her than excited. She was human enough, however, once she had resigned herself to the fact that it was better that she went to Peru than any other member of her family, to feel a small tingle of adventure at the thought that she was about to embark on something entirely outside her experience.

Though, strictly speaking, it should not have been necessary for anyone of the family to come to Peru looking for Audra. It really was too bad of her stepsister to take herself off the way she had six months ago, and to write but one letter to her mother in all that time.

Audra Billington was just turned twenty-three, only a few months older than Erith—but in experience, Audra was years older. Some people must be born 'streetwise', Erith thought—her stepsister was one of them.

She had not known anything of Audra Billington until two years ago when her father had married Audra's mother, Jean Billington. Both Erith and her sister, Bliss, had taken to Jean straight away, for she was a kind, good-natured and very caring woman. Only when she had come into their household had they realised how much their home had needed the motherly woman. Their own mother, tragically, had died ten years before, and neither was used to the small, inconsequential attentions that made up being cared for—the occasional cup of tea in bed, the 'I was doing some ironing, it didn't take a minute to run the iron over your blouse' type of thing.

Was it any wonder that she and Bliss had responded warmly to the woman, and very soon had grown fond her and were, in turn, pleased to do anything they could for her?

It was difficult, however, for them to extend any of the warmth they felt for Jean to her daughter. Audra lived in London, had her own flat, and it soon became apparent to everyone but Jean, who clearly thought the world of her, that Audra only ever came to Dorset to see her mother when she was short of funds. How a woman as gentle and giving as her father's new wife had ever come to give birth to such a hard-as-nails daughter was a complete mystery to Erith. But, since Jean obviously doted on her offspring, both she and Bliss had continued to try to like Audra.

Six months ago Audra had telephoned to give Jean the staggering news that she had met a man named Nick and was off to Peru with him. Jean had been more than a little disturbed by this and had quickly suggested that perhaps Audra might like to bring Nick to their home for a meal. But Audra had scoffed at the very idea, and a few days later she had departed from England, leaving her mother to watch every post for some sort of communication from her.

When two months had gone by but with not so much as a postcard arriving from Peru, Jean had begun to get distraught. Looking at her, seeing the strain on her stepmother's face as each day she watched in vain for the postman, Erith had started to grow angry with Audra for her thoughtlessness.

Then, three months ago, a letter written a couple of weeks previously had arrived from Peru, addressed to both Hector and Jean Carter.

As letters went, it was not long, but the news it contained was sufficient to make Jean look even more worried. For, with no mention whatsoever of Nick, the man she had left England with, Audra had written to say she was now engaged to some man who went by the name of Filipo. She and Filipo, it seemed, were at present visiting her fiancé's uncle at his farm, a hacienda in a place called Jahara which was about an hour and a half's drive from Cuzco. That was about the sum total of Audra's missive, and as the next few weeks went by, and Jean, with no return address to write to, again started to watch every post for more news of her daughter, Erith started to have worries of her own.

First she heard that the firm she worked for was in financial difficulty. Then, to confirm that what they had been hearing over the next month was not just exaggerated rumours, redundancy notices were handed out.

Erith received her redundancy notice saying that her secretarial job would soon be at an end on the same day that her dear sister Bliss fell ill with what was later diagnosed as pneumonia. It was a particularly bad bout of pneumonia, and the fact that she would soon be without a job faded into insignificance for Erith as terror gripped her that Bliss might lose her battle for life when her illness reached crisis point.

But Bliss, to everyone's great relief, pulled through and was soon sitting up and wanting to leave her room. 'You stay just where you are, young lady!' Erith, a year older, looked at her Titian-haired, twenty-one-year-old sister to tell her severely. And, smiling into her large green eyes while she studied her porcelain complexion, Erith, entirely forgetful that she shared the same Titian hair, large green eyes and perfect complexion, thought her sister beautiful. 'After the fright you've given us, you're not going anywhere until Dr Lawton says you can.'

A week later their anxieties over Bliss had vastly lessened, and Erith was again noticing that the strain was back on her stepmother's face. She supposed it should have not come as any surprise to her when her father sought her out to say that he was very worried that Jean might have a breakdown unless something was done to relieve her of her worries over her thoughtless daughter. What did surprise Erith though, as she agreed that Jean in her love for her offspring was having a dreadful time of it just now, was the solution he had hit upon.

'There's only one thing for it, Erith,' he had declared. And while Erith looked at him expectantly, he proceeded to astound her by saying, 'One of us will have to go to Peru to find out what the deuce Audra's up to.'

'Go to Peru?' Erith gasped. 'But...'

'But nothing, my dear,' Hector Carter had said heavily. 'Jean could get a letter tomorrow, she could get one next week, but that's what I've been telling her daily since she received that one and only communication from Audra we've had—and that was three months ago. Jean's just not believing it any more; and it's worrying her to death.'

'But—to go to Peru!' Erith exclaimed. 'Why, we don't even have an address! It would be like looking for a needle in a...'

'We have to try,' her father butted in. 'For Jean's sake, we have to try. She'd want to go herself, of course, but to travel as far as London gives her a migraine, let alone leaving the country.'

'Jean's a dreadful traveller,' Erith agreed, and Hector Carter went on.

'We must find Audra for her! We know she was in a place called Jahara, which we know is not too far from Cuzco, so it's somewhere to start.'

'Yes, but...' Erith was still staring at her father when she recognised his stubborn look suddenly. It was the same stubborn streak which both she and Bliss had inherited—a stubborn streak there was no arguing with. 'But you can't go,' she changed tack to tell him. Her father suffered from a dickey heart, and, while she knew that people lived quite active and fruitful lives with similar heart trouble, she didn't think the stress of going to a foreign country to look for his stepdaughter, without having any clear idea of where in that country she was, would be any good to him.

'It would only add to Jean's anxieties if I went,' he missed her point entirely to agree. Then quietly added, 'Which leaves you—or Bliss.'

'Bliss can't go!' Erith said sharply, not having to think about it. While it was true that her archaeologically-minded sister would give her eye-teeth to go to Peru, with its wealth of Inca history, she was just not fit enough to go anywhere near that distance. Erith's thoughts drifted off to how Bliss seemed to prefer her hobby of archaeology to boyfriends. In her opinion her younger sister would never have caught the pneumonia which had so recently very nearly killed her had she not, when caught in a downpour, been so absorbed in things archaeological that she had not only forgotten to change out of her damp clothes, but had blithely suffered several other soakings on top.

'No, she definitely can't go—she'll need a good few more weeks' convalescence before she goes anywhere,' her father interrupted her thoughts, and while Erith recovered to realise that somehow she seemed to have accepted that someone in the family was going to go to Peru, he added slowly, 'That leaves—you, my dear.'

'Me!' Even though she knew that, as he so rightly pointed out, there was no one else, it still came as a shock.

'Jean's going white-haired with worry,' he replied, and more or less as he'd said before. 'Someone has to go and send back word what's happening over there.'

Erith sighed, and thought it a pity that although Audra's behaviour had shown everything to the contrary, her mother should still think of her as an innocent young girl. A mother's love, she supposed, saw no fault. Since, though, Audra was so careless of her mother's love that she couldn't be bothered to pick up a pen a second time, Erith had to agree that something had to be attempted that would put an end to Jean's being so weighed down with worry.

It was then that Erith remembered how unstintingly Jean had given of herself to help her look after Bliss when she had been so ill—and suddenly she pushed out a smile. 'It seems to me,' she told her father cheerfully, 'that I couldn't have been made redundant at a better time.'

A week later she was in Peru. Last night she had changed planes to fly from Lima to Cuzco. This morning, after her brief visit to the city square, she had never felt less like smiling.

The day had started off brightly enough, she recalled. She had awakened early in her hotel room, and had even felt a tinge of excitement at the thought that she was here, in Peru. Then the seriousness of why she was here had all at once impinged, and Erith had realised that as soon as she'd had her breakfast she must enlist the hotel staff's aid in getting a taxi or some sort of transport to take her to the hacienda of Filipo's uncle in a place called Jahara.

Quite how she was going to find him, since she didn't so much as know the uncle's name, Erith did not know. It would, she felt, have been a help if Audra had thought to tell them Filipo's surname. It might not be the same surname as that of the uncle, of course, but it would be less vague if she could tell whoever she did manage to make contact with in Jahara that she was looking for the uncle of Filipo—whatever his name was.

First things first, though, and she left her bed to take a shower and to dress in a cotton top and trousers. She was about to go down to investigate what one did about breakfast when it occurred to her that, since whatever form of transport she managed to hire might, for an hour and a half's journey, prove expensive, she had better change some money.

It was not allowed to bring Peruvian currency into the country, she had discovered, so she delayed going down to breakfast while she sorted through her traveller's cheques. Her father had retired early, and money was not exactly plentiful at home, but, by a joint pooling of assets, they had managed to scrape together enough for her air-fare, with enough left over, they hoped, to cover her quest.

Taking a couple of sizeable cheques from the amount she had with her so as to be ready to change them at the desk, Erith was just about to put the rest of her cheques away when a smile suddenly tugged at the corners of her beautiful mouth. She and Bliss had been quite tickled, she recalled, when Jean had produced a little nylon half sock and, placing it in her hands together with a baby's napkin safety pin, had instructed, 'You can't be too careful, Erith. I shouldn't carry all that money around in your bag. Pin some of it in this to the inside waistband of your clothes.'

'Yes, Jean,' she managed, her grin, though, belying the fact that she was taking her stepmother seriously.

'Promise,' Jean had pressed, not taking exception to the fact that Erith seemed to think she was being over-cautious.

'You're lovely,' Erith told her, and obeyed a sudden sensitive urge to kiss her worried stepmother's cheek.

She remembered that promise up in her hotel bedroom, and delayed a moment more before going down to breakfast. Jean was much on her mind as she separated some of the traveller's cheques from the others and, keeping her promise, attached some to the inside waistband of the trousers she wore.

Breakfast, with the exception of coffee or tea which was brought to the table, was a self-serve affair. But, suddenly feeling an urgency to be about her business, Erith made short work of fruit juice and some cheese and toast, and went to the reception desk to enquire about getting some currency.

There was no problem in changing the two traveller's cheques she tendered for some *intis*, the currency of Peru, but while she was waiting Erith was attracted a few steps to the outer plate glass doors. The May sun shone in, and all at once she wondered—would it matter so much if she delayed setting about her task for just five minutes? Lord knew what this day would bring, but couldn't she have just five minutes for herself?

Her transaction at the desk was soon completed and, when a glance at her watch showed that it was still comparatively early, Erith gave in to the impulse to take a brief glimpse of the city founded in the thirteenth century.

No sooner had she stepped outside into the warm sunlight, however, than she was besieged by young women wanting to sell her anything from a hand-knitted cardigan to a strap to hang her camera.

'Not just now, thanks,' she smiled, and walked on down the wide street when a couple of other people emerged from the hotel behind her, and the young street traders went to approach them.

Five minutes, no more, Erith told herself as she crossed the road and took a left turn. A right turn and two minutes later, to her delight, she found herself in the city's main square.

Slowing her pace, she glanced all around the perimeter of the square, taking in the stone-built porticoes that fronted the various shaded shops. She looked at the wooden-built balconies above and breathed in the general atmosphere as pedestrians crossed the square, presumably to their places of business.

Thinking to take only another minute, Erith, attracted by the green-painted fountain, crossed to the centre of the square. Sculptured against the fountain was a tall and large white bird. Was it a stork? she was in the middle of wondering when suddenly, frighteningly, someone cannoned violently into her.

Momentarily shaken, a few seconds later Erith was shaken yet again when she realised that she was minus her shoulder-bag!

Feeling dazed, she opened her mouth, but no sound came out. 'My bag!' she managed faintly, as realisation set in that someone, and she hadn't seen who, so swift, nimble and professional on their feet were they, had stolen her bag.

The next hour followed in haze, though initially one young woman, seeing that she was in some distress, did stop to ask if she was all right. Fortunately the woman spoke English and, although busy with her own affairs, was kind enough to take time to go with Erith to the police station.

At the police station the woman explained what had happened and also that the Englishwoman spoke neither the Spanish, Quechua or Aymara which were spoken in Peru. With that, taking time only to tell Erith that they were sending for an English-speaking policeman, the woman left.

How long she waited for the English-speaking policeman to arrive, Erith had no idea. But as she waited, her spirits sank lower and lower. She calculated that she didn't need anyone to tell her that the chance of seeing her bag again was remote—that, even if she did see it again, it would be a miracle if the money it contained was still inside it.

As she waited she had plenty of time in which to regret her folly—to regret the self-indulgence that had seen her taking a sideways step from what she was there to do. Oh, what an idiot she was to go strolling around town with so much money in her bag! Where had her head been, for goodness' sake? What had made her think that Cuzco was any different from any large city? Idiot that she was, she knew full well that what had happened to her was, unfortunately, happening in cities all over the world—so why hadn't she kept her wits about her?

The English-speaking policeman, when he arrived, was charming but, as she had realised for herself, did not hold out much hope of her ever seeing her bag again. 'All your money was in the bag, *señorita*?' he questioned.

Thank heavens for Jean, Erith thought, and was able to reply, 'Not all of it.'

'Good, good,' he smiled, and, his eyes seeming to be drawn again and again to her Titian-coloured hair, 'You are alone in my country, *señorita*?'

Erith wasn't sure if he meant was she travelling with a companion or what he meant, but remembering Audra, she was able to reply, 'My stepsister is in Peru.'

'You're on holiday together?'

'Er—not quite,' she responded, and somehow found—while hiding the fact that she hadn't a clue where Audra might be—that she had told him that her stepsister was engaged to one of his countrymen.

'Her fiancé lives here in Cuzco?' he enquired, and seemed pleased to hear of the romance.

'Oh, no,' she replied, and because she hadn't a clue where Filipo lived and was afraid that the friendly policeman might want more exact details. 'Though his uncle has a hacienda near here, at a place called Jahara.'

'Jahara!' the man exclaimed, and seemed about to question her further, but Erith was starting to recover from the terrible shock she had received, and since she had told him all she could about the robbery she wanted to go back to her hotel, to be alone, while she got herself together so that she could decide what she should do now.

She was grateful to the policeman, who thoughtfully insisted on driving her back to her hotel. But once alone, back in her room, she sat on her bed and stared unseeing down at the toes of her shoes, feeling defeated. What did she do now? The policeman had said he would work personally on her case, but she couldn't see that he could do more than he already had.

Lunchtime came and went, but Erith was not hungry and still had no clear idea of what she should do. Again and again she went over ground she had been over before. There was no point in cabling home for more money—

there simply wasn't any more. All the spare cash they could muster had been gathered up to get her here in the first place.

Wishing she were back in the Dorsetshire village of Ash Barton with this nightmare behind her, Erith thought of how, on the day she had gone to book her flight, Bliss's temperature had again started to soar. Her thoughts had been more on her sister than on what she was doing when, intending to book an open-dated return ticket, she had inadvertently instead booked a one-way ticket only. Bliss's temperature had steadied once more before she'd realised what she'd done, but with everything happening so fast there hadn't been time for her to change her ticket—and Erith could only again silently thank Jean for the promise she had made her make which had resulted in the fact that, if nothing else, she had just about enough money tucked away in her waistband to pay for her air-fare home.

How could she go home, though? How could she go home without ever having so much as seen Audra, much less spoken to her? Despondently, Erith got up from the bed and paced about, as she had frequently over the past hours. She hadn't even started her quest—but if she did, if she did dare dip into her air-fare home, what did she do if she didn't find Audra?

She was able to see quite clearly that she could end up stranded in Peru without passport or money and with no way of getting back to England. All she would have achieved then, Erith saw, would be to have yet another very distressed parent back in England.

Thoughts of her father being distressed brought on worrying fears for his heart condition. At all costs, she then realised, she must try to hang on to her air-fare home.

Which decision was all very well, she thought a minute later, but how that was to be done might be a giant-sized problem. For just how, for heaven's sake, was she going to make the hour-and-a-half trip to Jahara without money? How, for that matter, was she going to pay her hotel bill? How, in any event, if her search for Audra took longer than the day or so she had anticipated, was she going to be able to stay in Peru for even a short while without dipping into her air-fare?

Erith had still not come up with any brilliant answer when a short imperious knock sounded on the door of her hotel room. A brief moment followed in which she was brought rapidly from her despondent thoughts, and then Erith, remembering how the policeman had said he would work personally on her case, went swiftly to answer the door.

It was not the policeman she knew, nor a uniformed policeman at all who stood there, however, but a tall, casually dressed man who filled the doorway and looked down at her from a superior height. As far as she could tell, he was not a member of the hotel staff, though, for, apart from his informal attire, no serving member of staff had ever looked down such a straight, arrogant nose, nor would so openly, thoroughly inspect her features.

That the individual did not seem overly impressed by the smoothness of her skin or the colour of her Titian hair was neither here nor there to Erith. He had knocked at her door, so it was up to him to state his business.

Why then, when she had just firmly decided that he should speak first, she should find herself breaking into speech was a mystery to her. The man had fair hair in which there were lighter blond streaks, as if he spent a good deal of his time out in the sun. He had grey eyes too, which to her mind, since all the Peruvians she had

so far met had brown eyes, put him in the class of being
a visitor to this country, like her, rather than belonging
to it. But even so, she suddenly found herself telling him,
'I'm afraid I don't speak Spanish,' and when that
brought forth not the smallest response, 'You've
probably come to the wrong door.' Then, her English
obviously not meaning a thing to him, *'Parlez-vous
français?'* she attempted.

'Fluently,' he drawled, and, as it suddenly hit her that
he understood both French and English, he went on in
fluent, barely accented English, 'And I'm sure I have
the correct door, *señorita*. You are Erith Carter, am I
not right?'

Somehow it came as a small shock to her to realise
that, apart from the fact that the man must be Peruvian
and not a tourist, he must be a policeman after all.
Though in all her twenty-two years Erith had never come
across a policeman like him! Her friend, the uniformed
one, must have put the plain-clothes branch on the job,
she realised.

That being so, she found a pleasant look for the aloof-
looking man, and told him, 'Come in.' She waited only
until he had ambled his tall, and without spare flesh
person into her room then asked eagerly, 'Is there any
news?'

'News?' he questioned shortly.

'Of my bag,' Erith told him, and as hope started to
die, she suddenly had the most dreadful feeling that she
had just made a most awful mistake. 'You are a
policeman, aren't you?' she questioned him quickly, her
eyes shooting anxiously to the door which he had just
closed behind him.

'You would do well to check first whom you are inviting into your bedroom, *señorita*,' the tall man gritted.
'Or perhaps,' he qualified, sounding tough, 'you make
a habit of inviting strangers into your room.'

'I do nothing of the kind!' Erith flared, instantly outraged by this arrogant man's offensive suggestion. Swiftly she skirted round him and went to the door. 'I don't know who you are, *señor*,' she told him heatedly, 'but I've obviously made a mist——'

'My name,' he sliced her off, 'is Domengo de Zarmoza.' He paused as if expecting her to have heard of him, but when clearly his name meant nothing to her, he went on to announce coldly, 'I am the uncle of Filipo Moreya. Perhaps, *señorita*, you have heard of him?'

Her hand, which had been on the handle of her door ready to open it, fell back to her side in surprise—that Filipo's surname must be Moreya was all at once by the way. Feeling for the moment stunned, Erith couldn't take it in that, when she had come looking for this man, Filipo's uncle, he had found her! More, that when she had always imagined Filipo's uncle to be around the same age as her father, this man Domengo de Zarmoza was much younger and looked to be somewhere in his mid-thirties.

Swiftly, however, she stopped being stunned and looked into the grey eyes that were so coldly viewing her. And it was then, as she paired his cold-eyed look with his blatant hostility, that Erith suddenly realised she had wasted her time in leaving England's shores. Because, as his chin jutted aggressively at the length of time it was taking her to answer, she saw that, although she had come to Peru to seek this man's help, everything about him was warning in advance that she would be wasting her time in asking his help over anything!

CHAPTER TWO

'YOU'VE heard of Filipo, *señorita*?' Domengo de Zarmoza repeated sharply, giving Erith the most definite impression that he was a man who seldom repeated himself, and, because of her tardiness in answering him, was irritated to have to do so now.

'Yes,' she replied quickly. 'At least, although I didn't know his surname, my stepsister wrote to say that she was—is—engaged to a man named Filipo...'

'Huh!' the tall man scorned, but had nothing to add.

Put somewhat off her stride by his explosive interruption, Erith stared at him for a few moments, but, when it became clear that he did not intend to follow up that scornful 'Huh!' with anything more, she got herself back together to ask a question of her own. 'Are you the man from Jahara?' she queried. 'Are you the same uncle who lives——?'

'Filipo has only one uncle!' Domengo de Zarmoza cut in coldly, and as that sank in, he went on crisply, 'The police inform me that you had your bag snatched this morning,' and, not giving her time to question how on earth the police had found him to tell him anything, he was charging sourly, 'No doubt you are penniless, *señorita*?'

His hostility, if not the reason for it, had not been lost on her before. But while she could still not fathom why—other than that he must have taken an instant dislike to her—he should be so hostile, neither was it lost on her that this aggressive man seemed to be implying that she must be after a handout.

20

For the second time in the very short time she had known him, he drew her anger. This time, though, instead of flaring up at him, she hung on to her control, to tell him proudly, 'As matter of fact, *señor*, I am not penniless.' She saw his eyebrows ascend a fraction, and guessed the fact that she could be as haughty as he had registered. 'For your information,' she went on stiffly, 'I put some of my traveller's cheques separately from the cheques and currency in my bag.' For further lofty measure, she added coolly, 'I believe I've about sufficient to pay my air-fare back to England.'

The man glowered at her, and she sent him a serene look and hoped his dog got fleas. Then she discovered that he didn't give a button for her proud arrogance as he questioned curtly, 'When did you arrive in Peru?'

'Yesterday,' she replied evenly, and couldn't help wondering what tack he was on now.

'And caught a flight down to Cuzco shortly afterwards.'

'That's right,' she answered, and unwittingly laid herself open for more of his aggression.

'So, after one night in my country, you want to leave?' he challenged toughly. 'This is your first visit to Peru?' he asked a blunt second question, having not given her time to answer the first. Erith started to get the feeling that here was a man who wanted things done last week and was impatient to leave things until the morrow.

'I've not been to Peru before,' she found herself answering anyway. And, as he rocked back on his heels and seemed to be expecting more, she discovered that she was telling him, 'I wouldn't be here now but for my stepmother's being worried about Audra.'

'Worried? Why is she worried? From what I've seen of the Señorita Billington, I'd say that she is more than capable of looking after her own interests.'

It was plain, since she had not mentioned Audra's surname, that Domengo de Zarmoza had met her—although Erith already knew that much. What else was plain, though, was the fact that having met Audra, the *señor* had no time for her stepsister whatsoever. Since, however, in the two years she had known her, it had seemed that Audra only ever landed on her feet, Erith did not think she could argue against his pronouncement that Audra was more than capable of looking after her own interests.

'It's natural that her mother should be worried. Any mother would be,' she told him sharply. 'Neither she nor my father have heard a word from her since a letter three months ago telling them of her engagement to a man they'd never heard of before.'

Erith fully expected another 'Huh!' to assault her ears. But instead, 'Why didn't your father and her mother come themselves?' was his sharply asked reaction.

'Because my father has a heart problem which makes it preferable that he avoid stress, and because my stepmother has problems travelling,' she replied tartly.

'So you were sent as their envoy!'

'As you see!' she retorted shortly.

For long moments they stood and glared at each other, and then, just when she was receiving the very definite message that, not without some cutting 'bon voyage'-type jibe, he was about to leave, he surprised her again as, his jaw once more jutting at an aggressive angle, he barked, 'What sort of envoy are you, to give up so soon?'

Instantly Erith bridled. She, who had spent her formative years in learning self-control over a short-fused temper, was suddenly tossing angrily back at him, 'Who says I've given up?' Most peculiarly, she could have sworn that the corners of his mouth picked up a trifle at the corners, but she was not in the business of amusing him, and went on to tell him hotly, 'The last address we have for Audra—in fact the only address we have for her, and not a full one at that, just the fact that she was staying at the hacienda of Filipo's uncle in Jahara—is yours.' Having come to a storming end, Erith belatedly realised that if she was to enlist this man's help—not that much help looked to be forthcoming—then to go for him in this bull-at-a-gate fashion was doing her cause little good. But, even so, she was not feeling very friendly towards him as, her temper once more under control, she asked him quietly, 'Do you know where Audra is?'

For long unspeaking moments Domengo de Zarmoza stared at her, then, evenly, he replied, 'I haven't seen her for three and a half months.'

Since, in fact, Erith calculated, presuming that Audra's letter had taken about two weeks to reach its destination, the time Audra and Filipo had stayed at his hacienda. 'But—you have some idea of where she might be?'

Hope nosedived when, after a second or two of staring into her large hopeful eyes, the tall man slowly moved his head from side to side. 'How would I know?' he shrugged.

'Filipo, then, your nephew,' she refused to let go. 'You must——'

'I am not in my nephew's confidence,' Domengo de Zarmoza cut her off.

'But...'

'Nor have I seen him since the day he quit his management job in my boat-building business three and a half months ago,' he told her stiffly.

That this man had a boat-building business as well as a farm was of no importance to her, though the fact that Filipo had left his job at around the time he and Audra must have been guests at the hacienda seemed rather significant, she thought. Though, with Domengo de Zarmoza suddenly gone all proud Peruvian on her, she didn't think he'd thank her if she started to pry.

She took a deep breath, and, for Jean's sake, and for the sake of her father who because he cared for Jean would worry too, she ploughed on to question, 'But you *do know* where your nephew lives?'

'I did,' he replied, to lift her spirits slightly. But they fell with a bump when he added, 'But Marguerite, my sister, tells me that he has moved out of his apartment and left the area.'

Where that area might be Erith had no idea—not that it mattered anyhow since it seemed that Filipo no longer lived there. Marguerite, she realised, as well as being the *señor's* sister, must be Filipo's mother. Hope spiralled upwards again when it dawned on her that, of course, Filipo's parents were bound to know where their son was living.

'His parents!' she said quickly, her eyes alive and urgent. 'They'll surely know where Filipo is now liv——'

'His parents are divorced,' she was again curtly cut off.

'But—but his mother—or his father—must know where he is!' She refused to be beaten. And when the arrogant Peruvian stood and merely eyed her coolly, she erupted, 'They can't just have—*vanished*!' and suddenly, as she began to see that she might have to return home and tell Jean that she could find no trace of Audra, 'Why,' she cried, trying not to panic, '*anything* could have happened to them!'

'Do put your imagination away, *señorita*,' Domengo de Zarmoza instructed her, a thread of amusement which she did not need lurking there somewhere in his voice. 'I assure you that if any ill fate had befallen either Filipo or your stepsister, then I should have heard of it.' Erith didn't know how he could be so sure of that, but he was going on, 'My nephew is twenty-three now, and has proved by his actions that he is no longer in need of a nursemaid.'

Erith wasn't so very sure that the uncle of the nephew was not being sarcastic and accusing her of having nursemaid tendencies. But, from the way he was talking—and he could have no idea of Audra's penchant for frequently exchanging one man for another, not that she had ever got herself engaged before—it seemed that Audra must be with Filipo, wherever she was.

So, ignoring his 'nursemaid' crack, she found more control, and a little tact, as she questioned, 'Wherever they are—they'll be together, don't you think?'

Steadily he looked back at her. 'Almost certainly,' he replied gravely.

Erith studied his strong face for a moment, thought most inconsequently what a very nice-shaped mouth he had and then, with more confidence than she was feeling, 'Then I have to start looking for them.'

'Without funds, *señorita*?' he was there swiftly to trip her up.

She tilted her head a fraction. It was now a point of honour that he should be made doubly aware that she neither wanted, nor took money from anyone. 'I'll manage,' she told him firmly.

For some seconds he stood watching the proud tilt of her head, and then, to her absolute amazement, he decided, 'You'd better come back to my hacienda with me.'

Erith was not sure that her jaw did not actually drop in her surprise. But she swiftly pulled herself together to tell him, politely, if stiffly, 'Thank you, *señor*, but that won't be necessary.'

'You have money to spare for hotel bills?' he grated harshly.

'I'm sure I'll be able to stay in some less expensive accommodation,' she replied, trying with all she had to insert some conviction into her tone.

'Huh!' his scornful expletive again hit her ears, so that she rather gathered he didn't think very much of that idea. 'On your own admittance this is your first visit to Peru,' Domengo de Zarmoza went on curtly. 'You have no idea, I think, of the problems you, who don't even speak the language, may encounter. You say you will start looking for them, but you have no idea where to begin,' he scorned.

Inwardly Erith blanched at the truth of his remark. 'I'll—I'll—er—find someone to help me,' she told him, and knew she was starting to sound very unsure of herself when he gave her a withering look.

'My family is respected in this area,' he told her sharply. 'I forbid you,' he went on, to make her hackles rise, though she could see he meant it, 'to make your enquiries of a member of my family when I've just said that I am willing to help.'

'When did you say that?' Erith challenged, her spurt of anger at his talk of forbidding suddenly negated. Unless she'd had a moment of deafness, this was the first she'd heard that he was willing to help.

'Did I not invite you to stay in my home?' he asked her arrogantly. 'Do you suppose I meant you to stay there indefinitely?'

This man was something else again! Erith fumed. No person she ever knew, in one and the same breath, gave out an invitation to stay while at the same time making it blatantly plain that he'd appreciate you not over-staying your welcome! But, as she fought a battle with pride that urged she should tell him exactly what he could do with his invitation, common sense stepped in to tell her she'd be an idiot not to accept his offer. Not that she cared a fig about offending his honour by making her own enquiries, but—as he had so truly pointed out—she didn't even speak the language.

She flicked a glance at him and saw that he was silently watching her as though aware perhaps of the battle that was waging in her. Erith took her glance away from him, and swallowed on a dry throat, and on her pride, then turned her glance back to him.

'You're—very kind, *señor*,' she quietly said the words that nearly choked her, the words that accepted his invitation.

Domengo de Zarmoza looked back at her steadily for perhaps about two seconds, then he opened the door. 'I'll wait in reception while you get your case repacked,' he told her.

Erith felt quite winded after he'd gone. Had she really accepted that hostile man's invitation? Had she any other choice? Not when he'd offered to make enquiries, she thought. Besides which, since clearly he was anxious to get rid of her—he'd only offered to help out of pride for his family's honour anyway—not to mention her earlier opinion that he was a 'get it done yesterday' type, she felt she could be sure that her stay at his hacienda would probably only be for one night, if that.

Stirring herself not to keep him waiting, she hurried round collecting her belongings together, and started to feel quite cheered. With his help, she could see herself returning to England before the week was out.

Taking one last checking look around the room, Erith moved to the door with her case and headed out to the lift. Her intention to settle her hotel bill, however, was thwarted when Domengo de Zarmoza, spotting her straight away, came forward and, taking her suitcase in one hand, propelled her toward the hotel's entrance with the other.

'I haven't paid my account yet!' she protested as firmly she planted her feet full square and refused to budge another step.

'It's paid,' he told her shortly, and made her furious by the fact that not only had he paid her bill, but that he was giving her a look which seemed to dare her to show him, and his honour, up in public by getting out her traveller's cheques.

'I'll pay you back later,' she told him in short undertones, feeling trebly furious that for some reason she was giving in to him.

His answer was to grunt something which she wouldn't have minded at all betting was some kind of Peruvian swear-word and, in total disharmony, they went out to his car.

It seemed to her that a good many of the motor vehicles in Peru, chief among them appearing to be the 'beetle' Volkswagen, had seen much better days. But naturally, she thought sourly, *his* car had to be speedy, immaculate and luxurious.

They had been some while on the road, though, when she realised that, since this man was going to help her, she should be pleasant to him rather than get rattled at the smallest provocation. As his guest she had a duty not to flare up at any given moment, she saw, and decided at that moment that she would henceforth be on her best behaviour.

That being so, she sought for some topic of conversation which might pass the rest of the journey in some degree of harmony, and ensure that she wasn't feeling like going for his jugular by the time they reached his hacienda.

She was about to make some comment in connection with Audra and Filipo, when she suddenly hesitated. For just then she recalled that, though she could not on her short acquaintance with this man remember him once being very affable, it seemed to her that his hostility tended to peak whenever her stepsister or his nephew were mentioned in the same breath.

Swiftly she changed her mind about the topic of conversation, and then had space to realise that she still hadn't got a clue as to how, when she had been looking for Filipo's uncle, he, Domengo de Zarmoza, had found her.

'How on earth did you know I was in Peru? Or for that matter, how did you know of my existence?' suddenly broke from her without preamble. 'I mean, how could you have even known which hotel I was in—much less that I was in Cuzco?'

The sound of her voice suddenly erupting into speech, when since she had got into his car he had heard not so much as a peep from her, appeared to affect her host not a bit. For a brief moment he took his eyes off the road ahead to survey her with a casual look. Then his attention was to the front again, and coolly he replied, 'By coincidence, the policeman you spoke with about your stolen bag has a sister living in Jahara. Consequently, through his visits to her over the years, he just happened to know that there is only one hacienda at Jahara.'

'Ah,' Erith exclaimed softly. 'Yours, of course.' Quickly she caught on and worked out aloud, 'When I told him my stepsister's fiancé had an uncle with a hacienda at Jahara, he straight away knew I must be referring to the hacienda owned by Señor de Zarmoza.'

'He's not a policeman for nothing,' her host replied, and at the chill in his voice she knew she had put her foot in it again, and that this man very definitely objected to any suggestion that Audra and his nephew were engaged.

Erith fell silent and refrained from asking whether her policeman friend had contacted him after he had driven her back to her hotel, for clearly he had. What exactly Domengo de Zarmoza had got against Filipo being engaged to her stepsister, though, she didn't know.

Perhaps he wanted Filipo to marry a Peruvian woman? she pondered. Perhaps, having met Audra, he just didn't like her? That was no reason to be so hostile when the match was mentioned, though, was it? It was impossible for everyone to take to all new members introduced into the family anyway, she'd have thought, though, from what she had seen of her host, she would have said he was above being petty-minded anyhow.

Maybe it wasn't that he had taken such an instant dislike to Audra, but that, having met her, he was very much attracted to her, and was against the match on that basis, she cogitated as the car sped on through picturesque countryside of mountains covered in greenery. She took a sideways look at him and, although Audra was never short of admirers, Erith just could not see this good-looking Peruvian as one of them. Why, she could not have said. It was just that there was something about him that seemed to say he was a bit particular about his women. Somehow she just could not see Audra, for all her blonde charms, attracting him.

The car had travelled a few more miles when, with a sudden jolt, Erith realised that her thinking of him being attracted to Audra was way off course anyway. Quite obviously, the man must have a wife.

She was unable to explain why that should jolt her so, but, shrugging away that odd feeling and deciding that jet-lag had a lot to answer for, she again swiftly broke the silence.

'Er—did you phone your wife?' she asked quickly, realising that he had probably done so while she was in her hotel room getting her case packed.

Idly he turned his head and looked at her down his arrogant nose. 'My wife?' he queried, and suddenly Erith could have hit him.

'Will Señora de Zarmoza mind my coming to stay?' she hung on to her self-control to question through stiff lips.

'I, *señorita*,' he drawled loftily as he looked to the front once more, 'am not married.'

Erith fell silent. There was no doubting from the virile look of him that, particular though he might be, he was not short on experience of her sex. So... Abruptly she cut her thinking off in mid-air. Good grief, why was she thinking this way? She wasn't interested in the wretched man, or his love-life, for heaven's sake!

They had turned off the main road and were travelling in some of the most beautiful countryside, where wild thistles flourished healthily alongside the most magnificent huge clumps of glorious yellow broom Erith had ever seen, when her host took another minor road. By this time she had forgotten any angry feelings she had against him, and just sat there absolutely entranced.

'It's beautiful here!' she involuntarily breathed, but was in such rapture over the valley they were now travelling in and which nestled in mountains of varying shades of green that she had not time to look at him.

'I like it,' he stated quietly, and his tone was the friendliest she had heard from him yet. She swiftly turned her head to look at him.

He flicked a grey-eyed glance at her, but his look was soon back on the road. That glance, though, had been

sufficient for Erith, in an isolated moment of sudden
empathy with him, to know that that word 'like' was a
vast understatement. He *loved* this place Jahara, she
knew he did, it meant everything to him. Where he had
his boat-building business she had no idea, but one thing
she felt was certain—wherever it might be, or however
far he had to travel to reach it, his hacienda at Jahara
was the only spot he would ever want to live.

The car slowed its pace, and he negotiated it round
some twists and turns as they travelled upwards, and a
short while later Domengo de Zarmoza drove through
a white-painted archway and on to a cobblestoned
courtyard. 'Welcome to Hacienda de Zarmoza,' he told
her formally, as he drew up outside a large and quite
magnificent white-painted one-storeyed building. Great
splashes of bougainvillaea of deep pink and purple
covered sizeable parts of the outer wall and, while feeling
slightly overwhelmed at even more beauty, Erith received a general impression that the Señor de Zarmoza
was a very wealthy man.

Either the farm or the boat business was doing well,
she thought briefly as she got out of the car. Although
somewhere along the way she had formed the notion
that the hacienda had been in the Zarmoza family for
years.

With her host toting her case, Erith went with him
through another long archway. A kind of odd job man
was at work over by a large swimming pool, she noticed.
But she had small time to notice much more than that
flowers seemed to abound in the borders of a very sub-
stantial area of immaculately kept lawn beyond the pool,
because her host was guiding her up three steps and into
the building.

From nowhere a plump and busy-looking woman appeared and was introduced as his housekeeper, Señora

Garcia. 'How do you do,' Erith smiled, shaking hands, and received a smiling exchange of what she supposed was the local Peruvian language equivalent.

Then her host was in what sounded like rapid conversation with his housekeeper and, as Señora Garcia went hurriedly to do his bidding, Domengo de Zarmoza turned to Erith. 'A room is being made ready for you,' he told her, and, with the charm of a seemingly willing host, 'Perhaps you would like to see a little of the rest of my house while we are waiting.'

'Thank you, *señor*,' Erith answered prettily. If he could find such impeccable manners, far be it from her not to do the same!

Her case was left in the cool wide hall while he showed her where the drawing-room, dining-room and breakfast-room lay. And all the while he chatted courteously, causing Erith to think, My word, this man *really* is something else again!

Fifteen minutes later he escorted her to the room she was to use during her stay. It was a light room, a large room, a room which, from another door which stood open, Erith saw had its own bathroom. The large bed had a carved headboard of dark wood, its darkness relieved by the most exquisitely worked hand-embroidered white bedspread.

'I hope you will be comfortable here,' her host said as he stood by her side and looked down at the top of her Titian head.

'I'm positive I shall be.' She raised large green eyes as she looked up at him.

He took a step away from her. 'Let me know if there is anything you need,' he bade her, and left her.

Someone had brought her suitcase to her room, Erith noticed, and while part of her thought she would be wasting her time unpacking everything, since she would more than likely be on the move again in the morning, she decided it wouldn't hurt to hang her clothes up. She began to unpack, but she was only halfway through when, after a tap at her door, the door opened and a pretty little Peruvian girl came in bearing a tray. *'Buenas tardes, señorita,'* she greeted her, and followed up with a whole volley of incomprehensible language which, fortunately, she accompanied with hand signs.

Erith went over and lifted the crisp white cloth that lay over the tray, and saw that as well as some delicate china and a pot of tea, her host, as if aware that she had been too bothered to think of eating lunch, had thought to see that she was provided with a plate of very appetising-looking sandwiches.

'Thank ... er—*gracias*,' Erith amended, and because the *señor's* thoughtfulness had lifted her spirits, she smiled and, after racking her brains for some phrase-book way to ask the young girl her name, 'Er—*como...*' she began, and changed her mind to try, *'Quién es usted?'* and hoped the dark-eyed girl would be able to work out what it was she was asking.

It did not take her long. One moment she was looking at her blankly, then the next second, to show a row of perfectly matched teeth, she was grinning, as she replied, 'Ana, *señorita*,' and went on her way looking happy with her lot.

Realising that she was quite hungry, Erith poured herself a cup of tea and downed a couple of sandwiches, then returned to her unpacking. Then, while hoping to be a model guest and not to go where she was not wanted, she opened the French doors of her room and stepped out—and was immediately awestruck. For the view from her room was breathtaking.

Towering mountains, green and fertile, stood guard across the valley, where tall trees stood in cool clumps around the landscape. There was a wooden lounger to the right of her door. Someone had thought to place a mattress upon it.

Erith, not wishing to intrude anywhere, but in any case nowhere near having had her fill of the view yet, spent the hours until it began to grow dusk in taking her ease in the lounger, in gazing at the view, and in trying not to let thoughts of Audra and Filipo penetrate. Domengo de Zarmoza had said he would make enquiries—he could be doing so at this very moment.

Erith guessed that her host might dine late, but she was showered and had changed into a crisp cotton dress when Señora Garcia came to sign that it was time to eat.

She followed the housekeeper to the dining-room, where the tall Peruvian was standing by a mantelpiece. He was showered and changed, she saw, and every bit as male-looking as she remembered him.

'Would you care for something to drink, Erith?' he queried, his grey eyes flicking over her while his use of her first name sent a small glow of pleasure through her. Apparently, since she was a guest in his home, he would not remain aloof.

'No, thank you, *señor*,' she murmured.

'Perhaps some wine with your meal,' he suggested suavely, and pulled out a chair for her at the table. 'Perhaps too you should drop the *"señor"*,' he added. 'My friends call me Dom.'

'Er—thank you,' Erith mumbled, and wasn't sure if she was thanking him for the offer of some wine, the invitation to call him Dom, or the fact that there was a hint there that he might regard her as more of a friend than an enemy.

The fact, however, that he might be extending the hand of friendship caused her to be a little reluctant to straight away bring up the subject of Audra and to ask what information his enquiries had brought. So she stayed quiet on the subject while they partook of a first course of asparagus soup, and told him instead that she thought his home was in the most delightful spot.

They were on the second course, a delicious fish which her host had explained was called *corvina* and which had been cooked in herbs and spices, when Erith, recalling how back at the hotel he had proudly told her that his family were respected in the area, suddenly looked up to query, 'Have your family lived her for a long time?'

'My Spanish great-grandfather settled in the valley many years ago,' he replied.

Erith smiled. She had thought he was not a newcomer to the area. 'So your relatives are all around Jahara?' she enquired pleasantly, and realised she had got that wrong when, taking his grey glance off her upturned lips, he shook his head.

'I am the only one remaining,' he told her.

Somehow, and for no reason, Erith felt a little shocked by his answer. 'Your parents?' she queried. 'Your father is...'

'My father is dead,' he told her shortly, and she knew she had intruded where no guest of such short acquaintance should. She was about to apologise, however, when the man who had called her by her first name and had invited her to do likewise suddenly added more evenly, 'My mother is French, and prefers to live in her native land.'

'Oh, I see,' Erith replied, but didn't see at all, and felt, in view of Domengo de Zarmoza's early shortness with her, that she couldn't ask further.

So she let the matter drop while she drank a little of the wine he had poured for her, and got on with the rest of her main course. She supposed his mother must have left Peru to return to her native France after her husband's death. She wondered if his father had died only recently, and suspected from the way Domengo had told her 'My father is dead' that it was so, and that his father's passing still hurt.

Pudding was a mouthwatering concoction of chocolate and coconut, and Erith was just savouring her second spoonful when she thought that surely enough time had elapsed now for her to put the question of what answers the *señor* had received to his enquiries. She owned to a small sense of foreboding before she asked, because, although he was acting the near-perfect host, she would have thought that if he had any information for her he would have given it to her before this.

'This sweet is out of this world!' she said for openers.

'I shall pass your comments on to Señora Garcia,' he replied pleasantly. Erith felt encouraged.

'Er—did you get anywhere with your enquiries, by the way?' she followed up a moment later—and could have hit him when he appeared not to have a clue to what she was talking of.

'Enquiries?' he queried, one arrogant eyebrow ascending loftily upwards.

Erith rapidly squashed her pugilistic tendencies. She had not spent years learning control for nothing. 'About Audra and Filipo,' she supplied. 'You said you would make——'

'You *are* in a hurry,' her host cut her off, an edge of irritation with her to be heard in his voice, she rather thought.

He wasn't the only one who felt irritated, Erith fumed. Of course she was in a hurry! She smiled as she clenched her left hand in her lap, out of sight. 'I should like to get home as soon as possible,' she reminded him calmly— but was promptly shaken out of her calm front when

Domengo de Zarmoza snarled, 'You have some man waiting in England for you?'

'No!' she erupted, wondering what that had to do with anything. 'But my father, and Audra's mother...' She broke off when she realised that she had already told him about her father and Audra's mother. 'Apart from anything else,' she changed tack, 'I should be back in England thinking of getting a job, not——'

'You do not work, *señorita*?' he cut her off arrogantly.

'I always have—since I left school,' she returned smartly, but had to add, a little lamely, she thought crossly, 'but the company I worked for are in financial difficulties and a lot of us have had to find other employment.'

'But so far you have not found other work?'

'I will,' she told him stonily, and, thoroughly disgruntled, she refused his suddenly charming offer of coffee and bade him goodnight.

She was undressed, washed, nightdress-clad and in bed when she cooled down sufficiently to realise that she had better stop getting annoyed with him before she began. Getting cross with him had got her nowhere, had it?

She thumped her pillow in the frustration of realising that, even when she had made a specific point of asking him if he had got anywhere with his enquiries, she still did not know the answer. If, indeed, he had bothered to make any enquiries at all, she thought angrily.

Why wouldn't he have made any enquiries, though? she thought a moment later. He might well, for the most part, be intent on being a charming host, but for all his charm he had left her in very little doubt that deep down he couldn't wait to be rid of her. And the quickest way to do that was to find out for her where her stepsister was.

Erith lay down and felt decidedly disgruntled at that last thought. It was no skin off her nose that Domengo de Zarmoza couldn't wait to be rid of her, for goodness' sake. He couldn't want to get rid of her any more than she couldn't wait to be gone!

CHAPTER THREE

FOR ALL she could not wait to be gone, Erith was still at the Hacienda de Zarmoza three days later. She awakened in her room on Friday morning and for quite two minutes lay there appreciating the glorious silence. For all of two minutes she experienced a feeling of utter contentment. She sat up, then got out of bed and pattered over to the french doors.

She did not go through the doors, however, even though she felt drawn to the view outside. For just then reality returned, and suddenly her feeling of contentment vanished. She was not here to enjoy herself, or to revel in the glad feeling which she oddly experienced at being here in Jahara. She was here at her family's bidding—she must remember that.

Just as she must remember, she thought as she turned round and headed for the bathroom, that her family would know no peace of mind until she had contacted them to let them know that she had located Audra, and that Audra was well and happy.

As she stepped under the shower, her thoughts dwelt again, as they had on Tuesday night and on Wednesday night and last night, on Domengo de Zarmoza's not directly answering her question of whether he had got anywhere with his enquiries. She would ask him again this morning, she decided, then began to wonder if maybe he considered her impolite to keep badgering away at him. Maybe, since he had told her definitely that he would make enquiries, he considered she should be content to wait until he had something concrete to tell her, she mused.

She towelled herself dry and dressed in a pair of white cotton trousers and a yellow T-shirt, and realised he could be thinking her good manners were at fault if all she did was continually harp on the one subject.

Erith left her room and went in the direction of the breakfast-room. She tried to instil in herself as she went the cast-iron truth that, since she could be certain he wouldn't be dragging his feet on this issue which would ultimately see her out from under his roof, she must resign herself to patience. She reached the breakfast-room having decided that, instead of putting the same question to him every moment of the day, for a change she would wait until he told her what information his enquiries had brought.

One thing was positive, at any rate, she thought as she turned the handle of the door; he would not be sitting idly doing nothing. She went into the breakfast-room, then, suddenly and inexplicably, was assaulted by a feeling of shyness and stopped dead.

'Ah, good morning, Erith!' The tall Peruvian lowered the paper he was reading, as he had done yesterday and the day before, when the sound of her entering the room penetrated. 'You're an early riser, I've noticed,' he remarked pleasantly as he stood, then moved to pull out a chair at the table for her.

'Er—yes. Do you mind?' she asked, and as she looked up at him and he stared down into her green eyes she got herself together, banished any ridiculous notion that she had felt shy for so much as an instant, for pity's sake, and added, 'What I meant was that I shouldn't like to disturb this time of the day for you if you enjoy solitude to start your day.'

'What a pretty-mannered young woman you are,' he complimented her and, having seen to it that she was seated, returned to his own chair. He did not, however, take up his paper again, but poured her a cup of piping hot coffee from an obviously freshly brewed pot. 'I am charmed to have you as my breakfast-time companion,' he added.

If he was charmed, then so too was Erith. There was no thought in her head then, nor as Señora Garcia came and went attending to their mealtime needs, to so much as hint that she had a need to know what fruit, if any, his enquiries had borne.

Indeed, so charmed by him was she and by the odd anecdote or two which he shared with her—for he at no time reached for his newspaper—that breakfast was all but over before Erith came to. It was then that she surfaced, to be plagued by the thought that, since she was here at her father and Jean's behest, she ought to be doing something other than sitting here making pleasant conversation with her host.

'Señor...' she began, thinking to brave his displeasure anyway and ask about his enquiries—only he interrupted her.

'Domengo—if you must,' he scolded her lightly, 'but not "señor".'

Erith smiled; she couldn't help it, 'Dom,' she obliged, and actually thought her heart skipped a beat when suddenly he smiled. Heavens! she thought faintly, and was all at once so overwhelmed by him, his charm, and his smile, that she forgot entirely what she had been going to say.

She still had not remembered when, his smile gone but his expression as he glanced at her pleasant, he questioned, 'Would it please you to come for a look around the estate this morning?'

Would it? She'd love it! She had, over the last few days, walked all around the lawns and gardens near to the house, but, she owned, she was itching to see more. Though, while trying to be a perfect guest, she was conscious that she mustn't encroach on the time Dom spent in his office working on his boat designs.

So, 'You must have lots of more important things you want to do than show me around,' she felt she should answer.

'You do not wish to come?' he queried swiftly.

'Oh, no!' she answered rapidly. 'It's just that...' Abruptly, as a grin this time spread across his good-looking features, Erith broke off. She mentally added 'crafty' to 'charming' when describing him, and tried not to burst out laughing—though the way his look stayed, as if in some fascination, at the upturned corners of her mouth, she rather thought she had given away that she was amused. 'Thank you,' she accepted quietly.

To start with they walked to the outbuildings at the hacienda. 'Do you ride?' Dom enquired, as he showed her the stables where several magnificent specimens of horseflesh were being lovingly attended to by a groom.

'No,' she replied, and doubted, even if she did ride, that she would ever be that good a horsewoman as to stay on the back of one of those speedy-looking beasts once they got going.

From there Dom pointed out a building where various pieces of farm machinery were kept. Then, maybe because she didn't ride, he took her to a set of garages, then handed her into a four-wheel-drive vehicle. It was in this vehicle that he took her on a guided tour of his land.

It was on that tour that any last misgivings about taking up his time finally left her. She had nursed doubts that on this her third day at his home, because she was his guest—however much unwanted—he felt he must take time off to see that she didn't get bored. But, as they drove through an area where corn, wheat, barley and beans grew, Erith knew, as she had known since Tuesday, that her host loved this place Jahara. It was a joy to him to be able to drive around it and to point out to her everything that there was to be seen.

'It seems as if everything and anything can grow here,' she offered up an opinion at one point.

'Jahara is one of the most prosperous valleys in the area,' Dom told her easily, adding, 'It was so even in Inca times.' He stopped the vehicle and they both got out.

Erith looked about her in rapt silence. Dom had spoken of farming way back in Inca times—what a wealth of history this place must have!

She walked side by side with him, stopping close by a brook which, after some way, rippled into a clear, clean, shining river. Under the shade of a eucalyptus tree she stopped and looked about, and knew in that instant that there was magic in this place. No wonder Dom loved it! She felt that she could love it too—as if, if she stayed here too long, it would so enchant her that she would never want to leave.

'It's—more than beautiful!' broke from her suddenly and involuntarily.

'You find it so?'

Erith dragged her glance back from where a herd of alpaca were grazing contentedly. 'Who couldn't?' she smiled, then wondered what she'd said, for there was no answering smile.

'My mother, for one,' he said curtly. 'She couldn't stand it here!'

Erith knew that she had somehow soured his mood when, without waiting for her, he turned and went striding towards the vehicle they were using.

She followed him and took the passenger seat, and recalled how he had told her that his mother lived in France. She had thought then that she had only returned to France after his father had died, but had that been so? Or was the truth that Señora de Zarmoza had been so unable to stand life at Jahara that she had left *before* his father had died? It was one of those questions that one couldn't ask. Even if she knew him well, and Erith guessed that there were few who did, she didn't think she could ask such a question.

Which left her on that journey back to the house—for she knew that her tour of the estate was over—knowing that there was a little mystery here of which she was never likely to know the ins and outs. What she did know, though, bearing in mind that Dom's tone had been short with her when he had spoken of his father's being dead, was that he in all probability had loved his father very much, and would not have taken it kindly if his mother had chosen to leave.

'Thank you for taking the time to show me around your property,' Erith broke the silence as he stopped the vehicle by the garage doors prior to putting it away.

A grunt of sorts was her reply. She decided he was charming when he was charming, but that he would be best getting over his sour mood by himself. He had opened the garage doors and was coming back to the driver's seat when she hopped out of the vehicle. She was on her way when she became aware that since the vehicle had not yet started up, he must be watching her. She kept on walking.

She had the swimming pool in her sights when Dom caught her up. She did not falter in her stride, but, because she just did not feel any animosity in her for him just then, she sent him a half-smile of thanks as, on reaching the house, he opened the outer door and stood back to allow her to enter.

His face was expressionless, she observed, so she could not guess at what he might be thinking. As she stepped into the hall, however, a man in police uniform got up from one of the chairs in the hall, causing her to forget everything else. For while Erith spotted that in one hand the policeman held his uniform hat, she immediately recognised that in his other hand he held her bag—the bag which had been snatched from her and which she had thought never to see again.

'My bag!' she exclaimed, and while she went urgently forward Señora Garcia appeared from nowhere, and everyone started speaking at once.

In no time, however, Domengo de Zarmoza had sorted everything and everybody out. Señora Garcia had been listened to and had gone about her business, and he had by placing a hand on Erith's elbow urged her to the drawing-room, while at the same time giving the policeman some instructions in Spanish.

A couple of minutes later there were three of them in the drawing-room, and her host was telling her that the bag had been found on some waste land, and was asking her to formally identify her belongings.

'It's definitely my bag,' she told him as the policeman handed it to her. Swiftly she opened it. Disappointment awaited her, though, in that, while her passport was still there, as were her purse and her wallet, both the latter were empty of their former contents. Gone was the money she had on Tuesday changed in the hotel, and gone too were the traveller's cheques which she had separated from those she had kept about her person. She coughed to clear a throat that was suddenly constricted from her disappointment, for even though common sense had long since asserted that she could say goodbye to the money, she realised that seeing her bag again must have given her some hope. 'It's gone,' she said huskily. 'The money's gone.'

Oddly then she felt a hand come to her shoulder in a firm touch of comfort, and she looked quickly up to see that Dom was regarding her in some sympathy. He had moved his hand away from her, however, as he asked, 'Is anything else gone?'

At first Erith rooted around in the bag to check. Then she realised that there was only one way to go about it, so methodically she emptied everything on a nearby table and piece by piece put back her comb, address book, a couple of handkerchiefs, and various other impedimenta. 'There's a lipstick and a couple of ballpoint pens missing,' she murmured, 'but they aren't import...' Her voice faded when on looking up she saw that Dom was not looking at her but had his eyes on the airmail letter she had brought with her and which was addressed to Mr and Mrs Hector Carter at Ash Barton. 'That's the letter that Audra wrote telling us she was engaged to...' Her voice faded again when any sympathy she had imagined seeing in her host's face vanished—if it had ever been there at all. Whatever, Erith knew that the stern expression he now wore was all on account of her having mentioned her stepsister's engagement to his nephew. Well, she'd be hanged if she'd apologise for that! she thought, feeling all at once mutinous.

'There'll be a receipt for you to sign,' Dom coolly cut through her rebellious thoughts, and, since she no longer had a ballpoint to call her own, he found her one of his.

Her rebellion had faded somewhat when an hour later she sat in the dining-room with him taking lunch. She supposed the fact that some gladness at having her bag back, albeit without her money, had something to do with it.

For his part, as far as she could tell, her host appeared to be in a more agreeable frame of mind than he had been when she had parted from him. Not that that had anything to do with the uplift of her own spirits as she sampled the *ceviche*, a typical Peruvian dish of raw fish marinaded in onion and bitter oranges and lemon which Dom told her Señora Garcia had made especially for her.

'It's delicious!' Erith exclaimed after sampling a couple of forkfuls.

'You sound surprised,' her host commented, looking amused.

'Somehow, I never expected to enjoy raw fish,' she replied with a self-derisory grin, and suddenly, to make her heart absurdly lighter, Dom's well-shaped lips parted and his head went back. When he laughed, it was a good sound, and she was careless this time that she had amused him, for when he laughed he was a much changed man from the sour individual who had driven back from their tour.

'We must try you out on some of our other dishes,' he commented pleasantly a few moments later.

Erith was all for that, but it all at once struck her that his remark had made it sound as if she might be staying in Peru for quite some time. And, loath though she was to upset this friendliest of atmospheres, it seemed to her that she should be stirring herself a little, at least.

'I think,' she began carefully, 'that I should be doing more about finding Audra than about enjoying myself.'

She expected his brow to come down. It didn't. She had thought, on past experience of how he reacted whenever her stepsister's name was mentioned, that he would go cold on her. But, to her surprise, he did not.

Though to her further surprise he had no reply to make about her stepsister at all, but took Erith up on the other comment she had made.

'You're enjoying yourself?' he queried, with not a trace of a cold look about him.

To tell him that the cause of most of her enjoyment was the beautiful place where he had his home would, she felt, even though she truly thought Jahara beautiful, smack of insincerity. So she waved her hands generally about, and told him, 'Who could help it?' She thought he looked pleased by her answer, but that was not the point either. 'But it's not right, is it?' she went on swiftly. 'I——'

'What isn't right?' he interrupted sharply.

'That I should be—er—staying in your lovely home— in this tranquil setting,' she replied hesitantly, 'while back in England my father and Audra's mother are so *untranquil*—so worried—and waiting for news.' It was there, the cold-eyed expression she had expected a minute earlier. Erith smothered a heartfelt sigh, and thought, since it seemed she had just landed herself in his black books, that she might as well go the whole hog. 'Have you heard anything yet?' she asked, and when all she got for her answer was an aloof look from down his aristocratic nose, she pressed on, with a fair degree of coldness in her own tones, she had to admit, 'Have you even begun to make your enquiries yet?'

Oh, my word! she thought a moment later, when 'arctic' didn't cover the freezing look he sent her. She was not totally taken aback therefore when, his voice icy to match, he arrogantly clipped. 'Did I not say I would?' Then, not giving her a chance to ask him what result he had had, he was getting to his feet and telling her curtly, 'I am working this afternoon. I shall see you at dinner.'

He was halfway to the door before Erith had got her breath back to say anything. And, while she realised that there could not have been any positive answer or outcome to his enquiries or he would have said so, she questioned crossly, 'And what am I supposed to do *this* afternoon?'

At the door he turned and, looking at her as though he considered her a tiresome guest, 'Rest—swim—take a walk!' he suggested arrogantly, and disappeared.

What do I do for a swimsuit? Erith fumed belligerently, and sat at the dining-table for a further ten minutes sending hate vibes after one Señor Domengo de Zarmoza.

When those ten minutes were ended, however, and innate fairness had prodded Erith to wish she had never asked that whingeing-sounding question of, 'And what am I supposed to do *this* afternoon?'

Dom was a businessman, a busy businessman. And even if her question of what she should do that afternoon had been meant more as a 'can't I get on and do something about finding Audra?' type of question, her host had not seen it that way.

Feeling a mite chastened that as guests went he must think her a bit of a pain, Erith took herself off for a walk.

Two hours later she skirted the swimming pool and, having spent a very uplifting time again absorbing the magnificent scenery, she went to her room. Closing the door after her, she was musing on the question of whether or not to write a letter home, when she suddenly stopped stock still to see that someone, possibly Señora Garcia, had stopped by her room and had dropped in a swimsuit.

A small smile played around Erith's mouth as she realised that, for all the antagonism that had flared between her and Dom at lunchtime, he had spared time to work out that, since her trip to Peru had never been meant as a holiday, she would not have included a swimsuit in her luggage.

Taking up the swimsuit, she observed that, though it appeared to be a touch on the large side, it would more than decently cover her. The small smile suddenly disappeared from her mouth as she wondered who the swimsuit belonged to. Was her host in the habit of entertaining female guests? She lost interest in the swimsuit and, throwing it down on the bed, she went and had a shower.

Dinner that evening was a cool affair. Quite clearly, the fact that her host had paused to calculate that she would need a loan of something to swim in did not mean he had thawed in his lunchtime attitude towards her.

'What did you do this afternoon?' he queried at one point, but, as Erith knew full well, the question came only out of a sense of duty to a guest.

'I walked,' she replied coolly, and, because guests had duties too, a duty to be polite, 'Thank you for thinking of the swimsuit,' she added in much the same tone. He inclined his head in acknowledgement, but that was all, and suddenly, when she was sure she was not at all interested, Erith all at once found she was asking, when she just knew that the swimsuit did not belong to Señora Garcia, 'Is it one of Señora Garcia's swimsuits?'

'No,' he replied evenly, and Erith thought that was the end of that. Then, with a cursory glance to her deadpan expression, he added, 'Marguerite is, I think, a little less—well padded—than my housekeeper.'

His sister's name was Marguerite, Erith recalled, and continued with her meal, realising that, unless the *señor* had a girlfriend with the name of Marguerite too, she had been granted the loan of his sister's swimsuit.

'If you'll excuse me,' her host excused himself when the meal was over, 'I have matters to attend to in my study.'

'Of course,' Erith replied politely, and, just so he should know that she wouldn't be hanging around for him to finish his 'matters', 'I'll say goodnight,' she said pleasantly, and, gracefully leaving her chair, also left the room.

Frustration wasn't in it, she thought when, back in her room, she owned that she was not a little fed up. She sent her mind back over the happenings of the day and, while a good part of the morning had been the most enchanting ever, when she thought of how her bag had turned up—minus her money—she felt quite glum. Quite plainly she wasn't going to get her money back. Which in turn made it equally and even more frustratingly plain that she was either going to have to continue to accept Domengo de Zarmoza's hospitality while he made further enquiries, or she was going to have to return to England straight away!

Erith eventually got into bed having realised that, when it ultimately came down to the peace of mind of both her father and Jean, she had little choice but to stay. For a while she had cogitated again on whether or not she should write to them. What was the point of that, though? She still hadn't any concrete news for them about Audra and, in any event, she still thought there was little doubt that she would be back in England before any letter she wrote would arrive. She lay down and tried for sleep, owning that she was not feeling all that happy.

Domengo de Zarmoza was not at breakfast when Erith entered the breakfast-room the following morning. Señora Garcia was there, though, and it was obvious as she attended to Erith's breakfast-time needs that her master had finished breakfast some time before.

'Señor de Zarmoza?' Erith queried, putting a question in her voice and hoping the housekeeper would comprehend that she was asking where her master was.

A whole stream of smilingly delivered Spanish hit her ears, which, when separated sounded as if *el señor* was at his *estudio*.

'*Gracias, señora,*' Erith thanked her, and again smothered a sigh as it dawned on her just how busy *el señor* must be, if taking just one morning off meant he had to not only work after dinner last night, but take an early breakfast, the sooner to be at his study this morning.

A feeling of guilt that she should be the root cause of why her host should have to labour so to catch up mingled with a feeling of being ever so slightly annoyed that she seemed to be getting precisely nowhere fast in her search for Audra.

Erith left the table aware that it wasn't Dom's fault that she was getting nowhere fast. Without a doubt he was pulling out all the stops in his enquiries the sooner to be rid of her.

On that unhappy note, she took herself off for another walk, where she tried again to find the uplift in spirit which she had found in her walk yesterday afternoon. But, though the view was as magnificent as ever, somehow she could not recapture yesterday's mood.

She returned to the house and, while wondering if she could do anything to help the housekeeper, rather guessed that any such offer would be frowned on by the owner of the hacienda. She might have asked anyway when Señora Garcia, somehow knowing that she was back from her walk, came and brought her coffee. The housekeeper's reaction, however, when, having forgotten a spoon, Erith promptly got up to go and get one herself, was to tell her that the señor was not the only one who would frown on any offer of help.

'No, no, no!' the housekeeper exclaimed in sudden alarm, and for all her plump size she went swiftly away before Erith could move from the spot. It was the maid Ana, though, who returned with the forgotten spoon.

Once she'd had her coffee, Erith donned the borrowed swimsuit and tested out the pool—and had to admit that she enjoyed herself. Any uplift of spirits she had found from the freedom and physical exercise went plummeting from her, though, when at lunchtime she discovered that she was to have her meal alone.

Not that she wanted to take her lunch with the wretched man, she thought irritatedly, having sorted out from Señora Garcia's jumble of words that Dom was having a working lunch, but there were things she wanted to ask him!

The things she wanted to ask him were all connected with the reason why she was there in the first place. And, even though she was fully aware that he must be up to his eyes in work, when two hours went by since lunch was over and although she had stayed round about she had seen nothing of him, Erith formed the view that it was about time she took some action.

Her first action, however, was to go looking for Señora Garcia. As it turned out, it was Ana whom she found, but she could just as well put her question to Ana.

'Estudio, por favor?' she asked her with a smile, and had her smile returned as Ana caught on, turned round, and led the way out of the house. Then she took her across a cobbled area and around a corner, and halted at what looked to be a purpose-built white-painted building. *'Gracias*, Ana,' Erith thanked her as the maid started to walk away.

Erith took a deep breath and, while scolding herself that she'd got nothing to be nervous about, for heaven's sake, knocked on the strong wooden outer door.

'Entre!' a voice she knew instructed, and Erith took hold of the door-handle and turned it.

The room she entered seemed on first sight to be filled with every up-to-date computer-type machine available. Domengo de Zarmoza was seated with his back to her in front of one such machine and appeared engrossed in his work.

Erith stayed silently by while he tapped in what seemed to be some sort of complicated mathematical calculation, and observed that as well as the other modern machinery, there was place in his workroom for a good old-fashioned draughtsman's drawing-board. This, she gathered, was where Domengo designed his boats.

His fingers on the keyboard were suddenly still and, aware all the time that someone had obeyed his summons to 'Come in'—at least that was what Erith hoped his 'Entre!' had been all about—he turned his head and saw her.

'Erith!' he exclaimed, and got up from his chair, and for all she clearly was not the person he had expected to see, she could tell from the pleased, surprised look on his face that he was not annoyed that she had come to seek him out.

Suddenly, and most ridiculously, all at once she discovered that she was, for the second time since knowing this man, suffering a most unexpected bout of shyness. Tosh! she scorned bracingly, but as she looked up into his steady grey eyes that shyness—or whatever it might be—had caused her voice to sound a shade husky as, she apologised, 'I'm—sorry to interrupt your work.'

'It was about time I took a break,' he told her with some charm. 'I thought you were Ana or Señora Garcia bringing me some refreshment.'

'Oh,' she said softly, and got to grips with her absurd shyness by bringing her secretarial self to the fore. 'That's *some* machine!' she exclaimed, pointing to a super de luxe-looking typewriter that looked as though it could do everything, including tap-dance.

'You type?' he enquired.

'I'm a secretary,' she told him, and was very pleased when he showed her over the various pieces of electronic and thermatronic equipment, and explained what each machine was required to do.

There was another door in the room, Erith noticed, and Dom had just finished telling her that the woman who normally performed secretarial duties in her own office next door was on holiday for two weeks when Erith caught herself up short. Nearly, so very nearly, she had impulsively almost suggested that she would be more than willing to do any typing for him.

Abruptly she reminded herself of the reason why she was there. Apart from the fact that if she was in any way bilingual then her two languages were English and French—and not Spanish, which would most likely be the language he worked in, she was not here to work, but to try and trace Audra. Indeed, the only reason she was now standing in this office block was that she wanted a few questions answered in that direction.

So, regardless of the fact that not once since she had entered his workplace had Audra's name been mentioned, Erith raised her eyes to her host's, and put the last question he must have been expecting.

'Have you received any answers to the enquiries you've been making?' she asked him, politely if bluntly.

As she should perhaps have anticipated, the warm and friendly light that had been in his eyes suddenly vanished. As suddenly too, it seemed he was a man who now considered that he had wasted enough time. 'You must have patience, *señorita*!' he told her sharply, and, clearly a very busy man, he went over to the computer he had been working on and stood by it, seeming now to be waiting only for her to leave.

'I'm trying to be patient,' she thought she should point out, 'but...'

'I will see you at dinner,' he told her, and Erith realised, if she didn't know before, that he was asking her to leave.

As things turned out, she did not see him at dinner. Not that this time he left it for her find out in the sign language and guesswork with Señora Garcia where he was. This time, maybe because he had personally told her that he would see her at dinner, he sent her a note. Would she excuse him, he would be having a working dinner because he was engaged upon something which he could not leave?

Erith felt mutinous as she went to bed. Strangely, though, it was not rebellion about how his enquiries about Audra and Filipo didn't seem to be getting anywhere that made her fume. It was thoughts of Señor Domengo Too-busy-to-make-it-to-dinner de Zarmoza that caused her to call on all her strengths of self-control. Never had she known anyone who could blow hot and cold so frequently, and rapidly, as he.

As now seemed to be habit since she had come to stay in his home, she thumped her pillow before she placed her head down it. One minute he spoke to her in warm and friendly tones and addressed her as 'Erith', she railed, and in the next instant, she was being given the short, sharp *'señorita'* treatment. Tomorrow, she vowed, she was most definitely going to get something sorted out.

CHAPTER FOUR

ERITH had not forgotten her vow the next morning, and was up bright and early. She had the light of battle in her eyes as, bathed and dressed, she went along to the breakfast-room. If her host, regardless that it was Sunday, had already breakfasted and started work, well, she knew where his *estudio* was, didn't she?

Her host, however, was not in his office but at the breakfast-table with some reading matter held up before him. His acute hearing ensured that he heard her come in, though, and even if Erith didn't know how he could distinguish the sound of her footsteps from those of Señora Garcia, it was clear as he lowered his paper that he had done so.

'Good morning, Erith,' he greeted her in a friendly manner—but she knew that that friendly tone could disappear on his next breath.

'Good morning—Dom.' She determined to start off right at any rate.

She took her seat and watched him as he poured her a cup of coffee and passed it over to her. He then smiled, but she wasn't trusting his smile any longer. She knew from experience that any sign of warmth from him could just as quickly turn into a snarl. When, though, thinking there was no time like the present, she was about to get straight in and, regardless of any hostility that might ensue, stick to her plan of finding out just what enquiries he had made on her behalf, her host, favouring her with a pleasant look, got in first.

59

'I have to go to Cuzco today,' he told her, momentarily taking her planned speech out of her head. 'I wondered if you'd care to come?'

His ensuing and unexpected invitation consequently sent her planned speech out of her head for much longer than momentarily. In fact, she had forgotten any idea at all that she had intended finding out exactly what had so far gone on when she told him, 'I should like that very much,' and the fact that she didn't have any *inti* to bless herself with forever on her mind, 'Perhaps I'll be able to change a traveller's cheque—I still haven't repaid you for settling my hotel bill,' she reminded him.

'On past experience, I think you'd be better advised to leave your traveller's cheques here,' he replied, and teased, his charm out in force once more, 'When I'm short of the small amount involved for one night's hotel accommodation, I'll let you be the first to know.'

What could she do? Erith knew it wasn't right not to insist that she paid her own night's lodging at that hotel. But with Dom being so affable, and even teasing her about an amount that must be peanuts to him, it did seem just then that she would be making rather a lot of fuss over rather a little nothing if she insisted. Besides which, he had offered to take her to Cuzco with him and, with him being so very pleasant, she somehow liked things that way.

It then seemed that no sooner had they finished breakfast than they were on the way to Cuzco. And suddenly Erith relaxed. All at once she began to enjoy again the beautiful view, the wild salvias and lupins that grew at the roadside, and the serenity of the whole area.

A kind of peace washed over her, and for long silent minutes she sat drinking in everything that passed by. It was quite naturally, as they motored on to drive by some grazing land, that, spotting the dearest-looking long-legged, long-necked animal and yet which stood no higher than a small child, that she exclaimed, 'What's that?'

'It's a baby vicuña,' Dom obliged goodhumouredly, and told her that it was related to the llama and how its wool was particularly silky. Then, the easy silence between them broken, he proceeded to ask her something about her life in England.

There was not very much to tell him, Erith thought, but conversing amicably with him while he drove, she was surprised how quickly they arrived in Cuzco. 'Are we here already?' she asked in astonishment and, as she looked at the curve of his mouth, then looked into his eyes, those grey eyes seemed to be mirroring her own thoughts that time went quickly when one was enjoying oneself.

At the thought that Dom seemed to be enjoying her company as much as she was enjoying his, her heart crazily skipped a beat. Which was why she was glad to be on her own when, in the next few moments, he parked the car, took up a package from the back seat and, telling her that he'd be less than five mintues, went off on his errand.

Erith owned that she had never in her life met a man like Domengo de Zarmoza, but the fact that the man seemed to be enjoying her company was no reason whatsoever to go into ecstatic orbit, she reprimanded herself. The exaggeration of the last 'ecstatic orbit' amused her—and consequently brought her back down to earth.

Ecstatic orbit! she derided—but she was still smiling when, in under four minutes, Dom returned. 'You seem in happy mood,' he commented pleasantly, and, before she could find an answer to that, 'Would you care for a trip around?'

'You worked so hard yesterday...' Erith began to demur, uncertain herself if she was saying that because he had worked so hard yesterday he must have time off, but by himself—or what she was saying.

She clammed up completely, however, when with a smile Dom set the car in motion. Taking a mountain road, they were within minutes, or so it seemed to her, stopping at a most impressive fortress. The walls of the fortress, which Dom told her was called Sacsahuaman, were constructed mainly of giant stones.

'How in heaven did they manoeuvre those huge boulders into position?' Erith exclaimed, wide-eyed and amazed.

'A very good question, considering that this stone here is said to weigh somewhere in the region of three hundred and sixty tons and that all the labour was carried out without the use of the wheel,' Dom replied.

Erith's eyes were even larger in her face as she stared from the tremendous stone in question back up into the grey eyes that looked and held hers for quite some moments. Then Dom was turning abruptly from her and leading the way back to his car.

For a short while Erith was of the opinion that *that* was it. But no sooner was she back in the car than any such notion that Dom, his mood suddenly changed, had rapidly gone off the idea of taking her a 'trip around' was quickly dispelled, when, turning to her with a pleasant look, he said, 'Since we were so close to Sacsahuaman, it would have been a crime not to show it to you. But,' he went on amiably, 'today is for taking in the countryside.' Erith smiled, and was happy again.

It was a beautiful sunny morning. It stayed that way as, appearing to be climbing the whole while, they drove over a rough mountain road. She observed more picturesque purple thistles that lived in splendid harmony alongside broom of the brightest yellow she had ever seen. They passed a herd of alpaca and then a herd of llama, and with everything so new to her Erith loved it all.

They were deep in mountain territory when, on such a sunny day and with such lush greenery about, she was taken by the contrast of snow-capped mountains in the far distance. 'It's stunning!' she breathed at one time, and did not need an answer, although as she stared at the Andean mountains she was aware that Dom had turned his head briefly to look at her.

A few minutes later her attention was taken by what looked like a whole wood full of eucalyptus trees. Then they were passing through a delightful Indian village community with a mixture of small dwellings, some having deep pink pantile roofs, other roofs being made from straw.

They were on a better road and were travelling alongside a stream when Erith was attracted by some Inca-looking terracing. Then, only fifteen minutes later, she noticed that they had come to a river. Whether the river was fed by the same stream she didn't know. 'What river's this?' she asked, and would have loved it had Dom stopped the car for a few minutes.

'It's the Urubamba,' he replied, but didn't stop the car. They crossed over the river, and it was about five minutes later that, having arrived in a town, he not only stopped the car, but parked.

'Where are we?' she asked.

'It's called Pisac,' he obliged, and asked, 'Would you like to see a market?'

Would she ever! Her face must be pretty expressive, she thought, for Dom did not wait to hear her verbal acquiescence, but in no time was escorting her through a cobblestoned street. Goodhumouredly he stood patiently by as, hardly able to believe her eyes, she watched while a nursing sow appeared from nowhere and then opened a door to a yard with her snout, and a whole tribe of piglets trotted out for lunch.

'Oh, how marvellous!' she exclaimed, and had more treats in store when Dom guided her around an atmosphere-laden market where all manner of articles were on display. There was fruit and vegetables of all kinds, and stalls selling jewellery near to other stalls displaying ponchos and sweaters, bags and spices, and all with a mountain backdrop.

It was noisy, and it was wonderful, and even the tiny tussle she had with Dom when he wanted to give her some *intis* in case she saw anything she fancied could not mar her enjoyment.

'Perhaps I might be allowed to buy you a glass of lemonade?' he queried stiffly, and perhaps a trace sarcastically, when she had firmly told him that although she liked a lot of what she saw, she didn't want to buy anything.

'Would you allow me to buy you a lemonade if I were the one with the *intis* and not you?' she asked him solemnly.

'Of course,' he replied without hesitation.

Liar, she thought, but this day was too good to want to waste it in argument. 'Then what are we waiting for?' she grinned, and felt warmed through and through when suddenly his head went back a few inches and he laughed.

Dom took her to a nearby bar-cum-eating place, but since he was treating her to a refreshing drink, and since she was in Peru, she turned her back on lemonade and asked for something she'd seen on show called an Inca Kola. Its bright greeny yellow appearance when it came was a bit off-putting, but it was refreshing just the same.

Dom had finished his drink and Erith, while knowing that they would now start making tracks back to Jahara, realised that she could not make her Inca Kola last any longer. Why she should want to was a bit vague in her mind. Though she rather thought it had something to do with the fact that away from Jahara she seemed to be getting on well with her host, and, although Jahara was starting to take quite a grip on her, once they returned there he might quite quickly return to being sharp and taciturn with her.

'Ready?' he enquired politely when she had finally placed her empty glass on the table. Inside the next five minutes he was escorting her back to his car.

They did not return straight to Jahara, however, but, to her utmost delight, Dom pulled the car in at the side of a wide stream. 'We'll have a picnic lunch,' he remarked, and while a feeling of utter gladness welled up inside her, he went to the boot and took a picnic hamper from it.

Erith went with him across the small bridge that forded the stream. It was there, away from all traffic, and with the sound of the clean clear water bubbling and gurgling happily over the small rocks that lay in its path, that she helped him unload the hamper which Señora Garcia must have prepared that morning.

He'd meant them to have a picnic all along, she realised, as she nibbled on chicken and hard-boiled eggs. Was there ever such a lovely spot for a picnic? she wondered as she gazed about at tall trees that seemed to go on forever up the mountainside.

'The stream isn't part of the river Urubamba, is it?' she asked Dom when she looked up on impulse and saw that for the moment he had his eyes on her.

He shook his head and, his gaze going to the water, explained that the stream was called Cuyu and that it got its name from the two nearby Indian communities, the Cuyu Grande and the Cuyu Chico.

'Are we still in Pisac?' she wanted to know, as she looked at and delighted in this little spot that seemed isolated from the rest of the world.

'We're in between Colonial Pisac and Inca Pisac,' he replied, and seemed prepared to go on answering her questions all day if need be.

But suddenly, as Erith looked at him, she discovered that her heart was behaving in the most peculiar fashion. The words to ask him a follow-up question died on her lips, as all at once she found she was breathless. Hastily she looked away—and then there, in that enthralling spot, she realised that she had never, ever been so aware of a man as she was of him.

It was something of a relief to her when Dom made noises about returning to Jahara. She spent most of her time on that return trip telling herself that it had never happened. That not for one moment had she been aware of him as anything other than the man who, when he would prefer it otherwise, was, because family honour decreed it, having to house her as his guest.

'Thank you for a super day,' she found her tongue to thank him sincerely when they arrived back at the hacienda.

'I enjoyed it too,' he smiled, and Erith turned and, swallowing hard, went to her room.

It was in her room, however, that while she might deny that she had been affected by him in any way, shape, or form that day, she could not deny that she felt oddly nervous about him. Which, when she could never remember ever feeling nervous about any man before, made it all very confusing.

Erith showered and changed into a fresh cotton dress, but felt no less confused than she had done before. All she knew for certain as she went along to the dining-room at about eight that evening was that somehow Domengo de Zarmoza seemed to signal danger.

He seemed as quiet as she over that meal, she rather thought. That was to say that, when her replies to anything he said were limited to the near-monosyllabic, he settled for giving her a steady scrutiny, then lapsing into cold silence.

She should, she saw later, have realised then that her host was not the type of man to let anything fester away without doing something about it. But she didn't see then, and was left having to hurriedly find some excuse when, just as she was about to partake of a mouthful of dessert, he suddenly broke into sharp speech.

'Something is worrying you, Erith?' he demanded to know.

'Er—no—that is . . .' she hedged, realising that, whatever else she told him, there was no way that she was going to openly admit how confusing she found him. 'That is,' she went on, and suddenly, when she had barely given her stepsister a thought all day, 'have you any news for me about Audra?' she asked him.

She saw his lips tighten, and knew at once that he was not best pleased that she had reminded him of her stepsister. It was all there in the short harsh, 'No, I haven't!' with which he replied.

His harshness, the curt way he spoke, annoyed her. And, annoyed, Erith wasn't choosing her words. 'It seems to me,' she began tartly, 'that, with your enquiries revealing nothing of my stepsister's whereabouts, I might just as well return home!'

As soon as the words had left her she knew that her host didn't care for what he was hearing one little bit. Not that she was blaming him that no one knew where

Audra was, but, she guessed, when a frown descended on his brow, that he took her comment that way.

She was totally unprepared, however, for the rapid and bruising, 'You have your air-fare, *señorita*?'

'Indeed I have!' she erupted and, her pride stung, she was on her feet in an instant. Able to grab at only the tiniest morsel of self-contol, she pushed out from between stiff lips, 'Thank you for your hospitality, *señor*,' and without knowing she could move so quickly without running she suddenly found she was back in her room.

Her next action was instinctive. Four minutes later her case was on her bed and she was more than halfway packed. Another minute after that, however, and there was a sharp rap on her door.

She swung round as the door suddenly opened, and to her astonishment Domengo de Zarmoza walked straight in. She was still feeling far from friendly towards him when she saw him toss a look at the bed.

'Good!' he rapped. 'I see you're packing!'

Warm colour rushed to her face at his non-subtle hint that she had overstayed her welcome. 'You invited me here, *señor*,' she reminded him with what dignity he had left her with—and for her trouble suffered rapid palpitations of the heart when, with what sounded like a very expressive angry Spanish expletive, he strode furiously over to her.

Suddenly, however, his glaring expression gentled out, and all at once the fingers of his right hand were stroking down one side of her face. Then, he murmured softly, 'What a sensitive creature you are,' and while everything in her went totally haywire he bent his head and placed a light kiss on her lovely mouth. Erith was standing as though mesmerised when he pulled back, and went on to explain evenly, 'I've just taken a phone call. Apparently Filipo has been seen in Arequipa.'

'Arequipa?' Erith questioned as she tried to get her thoughts together. She hadn't heard the phone ring, but she'd been so agitated that that didn't surprise her. 'Arequipa's—er—south of here, isn't it?' she queried, having somehow gleaned that knowledge from somewhere. Then swiftly, as her brain started to wake up, 'Is Audra with him?' she asked swiftly.

'She is,' Dom confirmed, and as Erith at once realised that there was nothing for it but to break into her airfare, she came to an instant decision.

'Can you tell me how I get there?' she asked her host.

'That won't be necessary,' Dom replied, and as he started to walk away from her, he announced, 'I'll pack too.'

'You, p-pack too?' she stammered.

'I'll come with you,' he smiled. 'We'll fly to Arequipa in the morning.'

Erith was left staring at the door as it closed after him. Filipo was in Arequipa. Audra was in Arequipa. She and Dom were flying to Arequipa in the morning—and Dom had just, ever so gently, kissed her!

Erith got out of bed on Monday and immediately remembered Dom's light kiss on her mouth, and how she had fallen asleep last night with her thoughts much more on that kiss than they had been on the fact that today she would see her stepsister again.

A smile of gladness tugged at her mouth as she showered, and even though part of her felt guilty that she must be taking Dom away from his work, she discovered she was very glad he was making the trip to Arequipa with her.

She recalled, as she dressed, how Dom had told her that Filipo had left his boat-building business. Perhaps, she soothed her conscience, Dom was keen to heal any family breach that might have been caused when Filipo had quit.

Since she had no idea of what time the flight to Arequipa was scheduled, Erith did not dawdle but, with all her belongings packed, left her room and headed for the breakfast-room.

She thought at first that Dom, unlike yesterday, had not heard her, for with his paper held up before him he did not acknowledge her. 'Good morning, Dom,' she bade him quietly, hoping not to intrude too deeply into whatever held his attention in his paper.

Slowly, though, he lowered his paper, and at the stern expression he wore her agreeable smile faded. 'Good morning,' he bade her courteously, if not very invitingly.

Erith took her usual place at the table and knew then that there was nothing wrong with his hearing. He had heard her enter the room—no question about that. It was just that, where last night he had been friendly, this morning his mood had undergone a change.

She reached over to pour herself a cup of coffee and wondered if she would ever get to understand this man's moods. Then she wondered crossly why she should want to. Just let her see Audra today—with luck she would be home tomorrow.

She tucked into some fresh toast which Ana brought to the table and thought how her host had obviously got out of bed on the sour side this morning. Not too long ago, she recalled, she had been most glad that he was to travel with her, but, since quite plainly he'd had second thoughts, she could equally well go on her own.

Having finished her breakfast, she decided she had had enough of being ignored. 'Excuse me, *señor*,' she addressed his newspaper stiffly. Her *'señor'* was not lost on him, she noted, when, lowering his paper, he surveyed her with cold grey eyes. 'Can you tell me what time my plane leaves?' she asked in the singular when she had his full attention.

'*We,*' he replied pointedly, 'will leave Jahara in half an hour.'

Don't do me any favours, she wanted to tell him, but, evidently having had enough of her company that morning, he got up from the table and, taking his paper with him—to give her the impression he wanted to read it somewhere in peace—he left her to it.

It was on the tip of her tongue half an hour later, as Dom hefted her heavy suitcase easily into the boot of his car, to tell him that she would prefer to make the journey on her own. But that, she thought as she bit back the impulse, would be being argumentative for argument's sake. It was quite apparent that he had his own reasons for making this trip.

It was a silent journey to the airport. But when the thought had begun to set in that she might never speak to him again, it was Erith who erupted into speech when, anticipating settling her air-fare, she realised with a jolt that it had already been settled.

'How much is my ticket?' she promptly, and sharply, asked him.

She gathered that he was rather good at Spanish expletives as yet another angry-sounding one hit her ears. She knew in advance, anyhow, that he wasn't exactly euphoric at her insisting on paying her own way the whole time when, remembering to speak in English, he told her curtly—and cuttingly, 'The last thing I want to do, *señorita*, is deprive you of your air-fare home!'

'Message received and understood!' she replied shortly, and had time to lick her wounds when on the plane to Arequipa he buried himself behind another newspaper.

On that flight, Erith pinned all her hopes on ending any responsibility of honour which the brute by her side obviously felt for her, by being on another flight before too long and winging her way back to England.

Last night he had gently kissed her—today he was acting as if he regretted that kiss. Well, he, with his sledgehammer hints that he'd be glad when she flew back from whence she came, needn't think that she'd read anything into that kiss that wasn't there—if that was what the cold shoulder treatment today was all about.

Let him try to kiss her again, that was all—not that he would. Nevertheless, Erith was in the throes of delightful visions of him hopping around half crippled when a well-aimed kick to his shin had found its target, when he grunted, 'Fasten your seatbelt. We're landing.'

They arrived in Arequipa in the same brilliant sunshine that they had left in Cuzco, the only difference being that it was hotter. When Dom straight away commandeered a taxi, it seemed to Erith, since he was without his car, the obvious thing to do.

They were driving along, and Erith was nursing the thought that all she had to do now was to check that Audra was all right, and maybe get her to write a letter for her to take home, and then she could catch the next plane out, when she thought to question stiffly, 'I take it we're on our way to see Audra and Filipo?' For answer Domengo de Zarmoza took a long indrawn breath— which told her that he was more than a little off her today. Well, that suited her fine, she thought sourly, he wouldn't have to put up with her for much longer. 'Well?' she questioned, her chin starting to tilt at an aggressive angle—then she nearly dropped when he did deign to say something, and she heard his reply.

'We'll check into a hotel first,' he gritted sharply.

'A hotel!' she repeated incredulously, and with worries about money ever present, 'I can't afford a hotel!' she told him heatedly—and promptly drew *his* heat.

'I sure as hell hope you're not going to insult me by refusing to be my guest while you're in my country!' he hurled at her, to prove he could erupt angrily in any language.

'Such charm!' she hissed—and, incredulously, could have sworn that she saw his lips twitch.

Swine! she fumed just the same, and all the way to the hotel she wished she were on her way back to the airport.

How could she think of flying back to England before she had seen Audra, though? she fretted, and again went over ground she had been over before. Both her father and stepmother, apart from being distressed, would think it very peculiar that she had spent all that had been gathered together to make this specific trip to find Audra possible, if she then returned without having so much as clapped eyes on her. They'd think it more peculiar than ever if she proceeded to confess, as in all honesty she would have to, that when she was within an ace of meeting up with Audra she had decided to return home, her mission unaccomplished.

The hotel which Dom checked them into was tasteful, quiet—and expensive. Erith was forced to accept that her host—for that was what he still was, she realised— would not have considered booking into anywhere of a lesser—and consequently more affordable by her— accommodation.

'I'm on the same floor, should you need to contact me,' he told her as he gave her his room number. 'The porter will show you to your room,' he added, and while, solemn-eyed, she stared questioningly at him, 'I want to check if my informant has left any message for me.'

'He—she—your informant—they know—knew that you'd be staying here?' she questioned, and as it started to sink in that Dom did not know exactly where in

Arequipa Audra was—not that he had ever said he did—she was of the view that, since it was her stepsister they were talking about, she had every right to go with him to see if there were any messages for him. The frosty look he gave her, however, showed her that her presence would not be welcome.

Oddly enough, that thought so hurt that, Audra or no Audra, Erith thought she'd be damned if she would tag on with him while he checked out his informant. Without another word she left him and went, with the porter in tow, to the lift.

Her room was large, airy and comfortable. Feeling out of sorts with the world just then, Erith kicked off her shoes and went and lay down on the bed, pondering mutinously, would that lordly swine think to ring her room if he had any news for her? Or was she supposed to sit meekly by and wait for him to condescend to tell her what information he had?

For ten minutes or so she silently rebelled against him, realising as she did so that she was much irked, since she wanted to take some action as soon as she knew where Audra was, that on such a lovely day she was going to have to stay put in her hotel room until he contacted her.

Mutinous thoughts were still rioting in her head when suddenly and unexpectedly there came a knock at her door. In a flash Erith was off the bed and, feeling that this was it, went barefoot in her haste to answer the door.

Disappointment awaited her, however, for it was not Dom who stood on the other side of the door but a tray-carrying waiter. 'Your lunch, *señorita*,' he smiled, apparently knowing she was English before she opened her mouth.

He was in her room and had arranged the tray on a table and was on his way out again before she got enough

over her surprise to begin, 'But I didn't order...' She
broke off. *'Gracias,'* she thanked him, and knew several
things immediately—one of them being the name of who
exactly had ordered a meal to be brought up to her room.
Another, that Domengo de Zarmoza fully expected her
to kick her heels in her room that afternoon.

Why else would he have a meal sent up to her? she
fumed, and did not thank him that, aware she might be
hungry, he, as her host, had taken steps to see that while
waiting his pleasure she didn't starve.

CHAPTER FIVE

MOST likely because she had plenty of time to spare while waiting for Domengo de Zarmoza to contact her again, Erith spent longer than normal in getting ready to go to dinner that evening. He had sent lunch up to her room, but, aware as she was by then that certain courtesies were instinctive in him, she could not think he would expect her to dine in her room as well.

By seven o'clock she was dressed in a green linen dress that went extremely well with her Titian hair and made her green eyes appear greener than ever, and was waiting. She was not a little cross, as the next half-hour ticked by, that she had been virtually checked into the hotel and dumped. Not so much as a telephone call had she received from Dom to say what message his informant had left him. In her opinion, not to mention the curt way he had been with her that day, she had every right to be annoyed.

Against that annoyance, though, she had to concede that if there hadn't been any message left by his informant then he would not be spending the afternoon doing nothing about it. She felt it was pretty certain that if he had gone out that afternoon, then whatever he'd been doing it was bound to have some connection with following the lead that Audra was in Arequipa.

When at seven-thirty on the dot there was a knock on her door, Erith, who had been waiting with what patience she could find just to hear that knock, involuntarily jumped, startled.

Consequently she didn't think it at all surprising that her heart should flutter a little when, after taking a swift check of her willowy appearance in her straight-skirted dress, she went to open the door.

Why her heart should flutter again to see Dom standing there when she had been fully expecting him was a mystery to her. Although she had to own that in his lightweight grey suit, white shirt and silk tie he looked little short of terrific.

She saw, just as she had taken in him and his appearance, that Dom, with an admiring look in his eyes if she wasn't mistaken, was taking note of her, from the tip of her Titian head, over her slender but none the less curvy form, and down to her two-and-half-inch high-heeled shoes.

Somehow then, at the thought that he seemed to have an admiring look in his eyes, her voice, strangely, failed her. Not so Dom, though, and she realised that she had been wrong about the admiration too when, his voice even, he said, 'Good, I see you're ready to eat.'

'Thank you for lunch,' she murmured, trying for his even tone while at the same time trying to hold down her sarcasm.

His answer was to take her room key from her and lock her door. He then returned the key to her. Side by side they walked to the lift, and as he pressed the call button Erith gleaned that he seemed to be in a better humour than he'd been in earlier. Did that mean that he'd tracked down Audra and Filipo?

It was on the tip of her tongue to ask straight away, but then the lift arrived and he ushered her into it. Suddenly, however, Erith changed her mind about asking the question that was burning to be asked. Surely if he had anything to tell her then he'd tell her at once? And if he hadn't anything to tell her, all she would do would

be to stir his aggression again. Not that she was
frightened of him, far from it, but—most unexpectedly,
a most peculiar feeling of not wanting to fight with him
came over her.

She was still in the throes of wondering what the
dickens that could mean, when so far as she could remember she had never backed off since she had known
him, while they entered the hotel's dining-room and were
shown to a table.

Erith had acknowledged since her arrival in Peru the
discovery of a very experimental palate. But the feeling
of wanting to try whatever local dish might be on the
menu left her that evening, so that she was barely aware
of what she had ordered or what she ate.

'Have you rested this afternoon, Erith?' her host enquired affably enough, causing her to realise that either
she had been right and he was in a better humour, or
the innate courtesy she had noticed about him decreed
that he would not snarl at her throughout dinner—not
while they were in a public place.

'I don't normally require a rest in the afternoon,' she
replied, matching him for affability, she hoped.

'You don't normally live at seven thousand feet above
sea-level, either,' Dom replied pleasantly, and suddenly
Erith started to warm to him. All at once she realised
that it could be that he had deliberately left her to her
own devices that afternoon, and other times since she'd
been in Peru, so that she could rest, the better to ac-
climatise herself to this part of the world where the air
was thinner than she was used to.

Feeling much more friendly towards him than she had,
she very nearly asked him what he had done that
afternoon—then remembered how whatever he had done
had to be connected in some way with her stepsister—
his non-favourite subject.

'You have a sister, I believe?' To her astonishment she heard herself opening up a different subject—that subject triggered off, she rather thought, by the fact that the word 'sister' was still floating around in her head.

'It's true, I have.' Dom answered slowly, his eyes steady on hers as if trying to gauge what, if anything, she was leading up to.

'An elder sister?' she queried.

'Filipo, as I once told you, is twenty-three,' he reminded her, as though suspecting that she had forgotten but had wanted to know his nephew's age.

'So your sister must be fortyish,' Erith continued, with no idea why she was carrying on with this conversation—though she did have to own that she had felt more than the odd curiosity about this man and his family. And after all, he had once asked her to tell him about herself.

'Marguerite is forty-three, but she would not thank me for telling you that,' he told her solemnly, and suddenly, by the mere fact that he was parting with that confidence to her, small though that piece of private information was, Erith started to feel absurdly good inside.

'Thank you,' she told him, and with a smile that drew his eyes to the curve of her mouth she told him, 'I shall guard that secret with my life,' and loved it when, in that way he had, he tipped back his head a few inches and laughed. Erith coughed to clear a suddenly constricted throat. 'And—er—Marguerite, she lives in Peru?' she dragged her eyes from him to ask another question—any question to help her over this sudden trembly feeling inside.

'Again, that's true,' Dom replied, but there was something in his tone that seemed to be warning that he was about to take exception to her line of questioning.

'I'm sorry,' Erith volunteered at once. 'Am I prying?'

For answer, he looked long into her contrite green eyes. Then, clearly, she heard him state, 'You, my dear Erith, have at times a most charming way with you.'

For a moment she was stunned. Then, as her heart started to misbehave again, she doubted that she had heard what she thought she had just heard. She looked at him for confirmation, but he was busy taking a sip from his wine and she could not read his expression.

'I—er...' she said as his wine glass went down, then heard him give an exclamation of surprise.

'Why, I do believe you're blushing!' he added to his exclamation, his tone gently incredulous.

'Am I?' she asked, and had to own that her normally pale skin felt hot enough to be suffused with warm pink. But, not really needing his answer, 'Have you ever been to France?' she asked the first question to come into her head. Silence fell between them so that she almost followed it up with, why did I ask that?—but suddenly she knew. Dom had said his mother lived in France, and she was discovering that she had a burning curiosity about anything connected with him. She wanted to apologise for prying, but worried that he might think she was fishing for another compliment.

Starting to feel miserable that Dom clearly was not going to answer her question, and must obviously think she'd got a nerve, she reached for her wine glass to take a sip. It was then that she recalled what might have triggered her question. For she plainly remembered how he had said that his mother lived in France and how she herself had later wondered if his mother had returned to France before or after his father's death. She also remembered how she had realised that it was one of those questions one did not ask.

She returned her wine glass to the table, and because she could not bear the strain of the silence she had caused she looked across the table at the tall Peruvian. Then it was that it seemed he had come to some kind of decision, because then, to her enormous relief, not to say great joy, he was telling her, 'In answer to your question, Erith, I visit France once a year—at least.' Feeling that she had asked more than enough, she held down what would have been a natural—'To see your mother?' But, to make her warm to him again, Dom was going on, just as though he had read the question—and her restraint—in her eyes, 'My mother, as you know, lives there.'

'Does—er—Marguerite go too?' Erith found what she thought was a harmless question.

'More frequently than I,' he told her, and added, 'But then Marguerite is more French than she is Peruvian.'

'Is she?' Erith couldn't refrain from asking.

'I may tell you about it some time,' Dom replied, and when she wanted to know much more she could see that, even though he smiled, he did not intend to tell her more than he had. He softened what might have been felt as a snub, however, by bouncing a similar question to an earlier one of hers back at her. 'How about you, Erith. France is much nearer to you than me. Have you ever been there?'

'My sister and I——' she began, but stopped abruptly as immediately all sign of friendliness went from him. 'What...?' she started to ask, then realised that he thought she was about to tell him something in connection with her and her stepsister. 'I meant Bliss, my sister, not my——' Abruptly she halted again. 'You don't like my stepsister, do you?' she questioned a little stiffly.

'Do you?' he countered sharply, any warmth that might have flowed between them swiftly at an end.

'I . . .' she began hurriedly, but, because she suddenly felt totally unable to lie to him, she halted again. She had tried, and for Jean's sake had tried hard, to like Audra, but the truth of the matter was that she did not like her stepsister. But to tell Dom so made her feel she was being disloyal to Jean, and that made her cross with him, so she ignored his question and acted as though he'd never asked it. 'Anyhow,' she told him, 'you don't have to like Audra, do you? She's marrying Filipo, not...' She broke off again when she could have sworn that the man sitting opposite her had just muttered a very English-sounding, 'Not if I can do anything to prevent it.'

Starting to feel more angry with him than merely just cross, Erith drew a controlling breath. The meal was almost over, as was any hope of a return of any friendliness between them. She thought she might just as well go up to her room. Before she did that, though, it seemed to her more than about time that he shared what information he had gleaned.

'So what did you find out?' she asked him coolly, and had to take another controlling breath when he feigned not to know what she was talking about.

'About what?' he returned, his tones several degrees cooler than hers.

'About—my—stepsister!' Erith hissed through clenched teeth.

Her temper in no way cooled at the time it took him to answer. For all of five seconds, she was sure, he looked arrogantly back at her down his superior nose. Then, after yet another pause, he shrugged, then, as cool as you like, he clipped, 'They've moved on.'

'*Moved on!*' Erith exclaimed, any attempt to remain cool suddenly shattered. 'What do you mean—they've moved on? You said——'

'I know what I said,' he cut her off. 'They *were* in Arequipa, but apparently Filipo has decided to take your stepsister on a tour of his country.'

'Oh, no!' Erith gasped, and knew at once that this was the end. Apart from the financial aspect of it all, she saw that any chance of her catching up with them had just disintegrated. Her quest, she realised, was hopeless. 'That's it, then,' she muttered as she faced what was plain to see.

She was about to get up and leave the table, though, when her host, his voice all aggression, stopped her. 'That's what?' he questioned sharply.

'It's obvious, isn't it?' she flared in an undertone. 'I'll just have to return home!'

'Why?' he rapped back, his aggression out in full force, making her glad that their table was discreetly out of earshot of any of the other diners, when he accused, 'You've some man you can't wait to get back to in England!'

'No, I haven't!' Erith denied hotly when she had got her breath back from his astonishing statement—what had that got to do with what they were talking about, for heaven's sake?

'Yes, you have!' He refused to let the subject drop. 'Ever since you got here you've been panting to get back to your lover!'

'Lover!' she snapped in explosive fury. 'Don't talk rot! I haven't got a lover! I've never had a lover! And for your information——'

'You've never had a lover?' he interrupted to challenge fiercely, the look of disbelief on his face all she needed to know that, though in her view she had in the heat of the moment told him too much, he clearly did not believe the truth of that she was telling him. And that made her angrier than ever.

'That's what I said!' she stormed. 'And that's what I meant. It's the truth, but I don't give a button whether you believe—— '

'You're saying that no man has ever made love to you?'

Some of his aggression seemed to have gone, Erith thought as she glared at him. At any rate, he was now looking more incredulous than as though he thought she was lying through her teeth, she realised. She took a steadying breath, and had garnered some control of her temper when, for the record, she told him tautly, 'I've had my moments, of course, but I've...' Her voice suddenly began to falter as, her anger cooling rapidly, she became self-conscious at talking so openly about such a private matter. 'But,' she resumed when she saw that it seemed Dom was insisting that she finish what she had begun. 'I've never been to bed with a man.'

'Ah!' he exclaimed, but his exclamation was breathed softly and she could tell nothing of what his exclamation meant. If her anger had cooled, though, it soon became apparent that his fury was a thing of the past too when, as he had waited for her to finish, she waited for him to add something to that 'Ah!' But to her utter amazement he leaned back in his chair and commented conversationally, 'I've never made love to a virgin.'

'Y-you...' Erith spluttered. Then, just in case his comment wasn't just conversational, she thought she should smartly set him straight. 'You can take all bright ideas like that out of your mind right away!' she erupted—then saw, with no little confusion, that she had got it completely wrong when he became the one to look amazed.

Her colour was still high when, as blunt as she, he coolly told her, 'Don't delude yourself, *señorita*,' and added for good sarcastic measure, 'that you should get

to be so fortunate.' She was still cringing from the sting
of that remark when, dropping that part of the conversation entirely—just as if *she* had offended *him*!—he
deliberated evenly, 'It seems to me, that you are not at
all unhappy to have to return to your family and admit
to them that you have not tried very hard to do their
bidding.'

'Not unhappy...!' Erith flared, and was all at once
furious with him again. 'Not tried very hard!' she exploded. 'W——'

'Even when you've been given every opportunity
to——'

'What opportunity?' she heatedly cut him off. 'You
know how I'm placed,' she went on rapidly. 'Even with
limitless funds I'd be hard put to it to find out on my
own where they've gone to now! How——?'

'Didn't you hear me say that it's about time I took a
few days off, and that I'd use them to help you to find
your stepsister?' he cut her off.

'You never said anything of the sort!' Erith flew, and
was in the throes of astonished outrage at his last remark
when suddenly he leaned back in his chair and, after
studying the green sparks flashing from her eyes, all at
once smiled.

That smile, that something about his smile, sent her
heart flipping within her body. This is crazy, she tried
to tell herself, but there was so much charm to the man
when he cared to exercise it that, without having to say
a word, just by making his nice mouth turn up at the
corners, it seemed, he could negate her fury.

Swiftly she looked away from him and tried to remember what it was he had just said. Hadn't he just said
that he would take a few days off to help her track down
Audra? 'Will you?' She looked at him again to ask.

'Of course,' he replied. 'Would you like more coffee?'

Strangely, with so much on her mind, Erith slept soundly that night. She drifted off to sleep with the face of a tall Peruvian in her mind's eye—he was smiling.

She awakened on Tuesday to realise that she had been in Peru for over a week now and had not yet sent so much as a postcard back home. How could she, though? They were bound to expect Audra's name to appear somewhere on any missive she sent them, and would be even more anxious if she didn't mention her name at all!

After several agonised minutes of yet again wondering what she should do for the best, Erith decided to leave it for a few more days. Surely in a few more days she would have something to tell her family—then she could telephone. As it was, although they would be watching the post, they could well think there might be difficulties with the postal service at the present time.

Erith went and had her bath, and found that her thoughts wandered on to Dom de Zarmoza. She spent some time playing back in her mind all that had been said at dinner last night. She still felt a little pink about the ears when she recalled how, to her astonishment, she had as good as told him of her virgin state. But she passed swiftly over his 'Don't delude yourself, *señorita*, that you should get to be so fortunate' comment when she had smartly told him he could forget any idea of being the one to take her virginity. Instead she latched her thoughts on to how he had said he would take some time off work to help her find Audra.

Now, wasn't that good of him? She remembered how hard he worked and thought it was doubly good of him to take time off on her behalf. For a while she wondered again why he should put himself out to help her. It wasn't even as though he had any liking for Audra, was it? He valued his family honour, of course, but he had only taken her to Jahara in the first place on account of her claim to the police that her stepsister was engaged to his nephew. It could be, of course, that Dom was just being courteous to a visitor to his country.

No, that couldn't be right, Erith thought a moment later. From what she knew of him, she'd have said he'd say to hell with courtesy if he didn't like you. His courtesy, though, was inbuilt, she recalled, and began, as she suddenly found herself wondering if any of this meant that perhaps he liked her, to become more than a little confused.

When her heart began to hurry its beat, she knew that it had nothing to do with the thought that Dom might like her. Her heart had only begun to behave in that peculiar fashion since she had arrived in Peru, she recalled, so the thin air had much to answer for. In any case, it didn't matter a fig to her whether he liked her or not.

Her heart gave another of its recently learned flutters when half an hour later she walked into the dining-room and saw that Dom was already at breakfast.

'Sleep well?' he enquired pleasantly as he rose and pulled out a chair for her.

'Like a top,' she smiled, and, while not bothered whether he liked her or not, she discovered as he looked solemnly deep into her eyes and then smiled slowly, that she felt exceedingly good about life.

It was only because he was going to see to it personally that they met up with Audra and Filipo that she felt so good, she realised, and had a happy breakfast during which she did her best to explain to Dom the meaning of sleeping 'like a top'.

They were just finishing the last of their coffee when she wondered if she should ask him what he proposed they should do about tracing Audra and Filipo that day.

But, as though he had just read her mind, Dom at once told her that his enquiries were continuing and that they must wait to hear from his contact. 'In the meantime,' he went on, 'might I suggest that we spend the waiting time in taking a look around Arequipa?'

The idea had tremendous appeal, though she was doubtful that a man of his undisputed sophistication would enjoy anything so 'touristy' as taking a stroll around the city.

'I should like to, of course I should,' she told him honestly. 'But I'm not sure about you...'

'You prefer not to have my company?' he asked at once, the aloof person she had not seen for some time instantly back again.

'Of course I prefer to have your company,' Erith jumped in to make things right. 'It's just that...'

'That?' prompted Dom, though she was relieved to see that his aloof look was starting to fade.

'Well, that you don't have to take me about while we wait. I mean, I shouldn't want you to be bored...'

'Bored?' he took up, as though that notion was impossible. Then, every scrap of aloofness gone from him, he gently touched a finger to her chin. 'I have said before that you are a sensitive creature, have I not?' he said softly, and Erith was hard put to it not to swallow on a knot of unexpected and sudden emotion.

They first of all toured the outskirts of the city by taxi, and Erith was fascinated to see the cultivated agricultural terraces and canals which even in pre-Inca times were fed by the life-blood of Arequipa, the river Chili.

The next few hours seemed to go by in a flash, with lasting impressions staying with her. Arequipa, or *La Ciudad Blanca*, the White City, as it was known, was so called, Dom told her, because of the white sillar stone from which most of the buildings were built. Sillar was the volcanic material thrown up by the Chachani volcano which stood snow-covered and quiet and kept sentinel over the city with the dormant snow-capped volcano known locally as *El Misti* and at whose foot the city was built. *El Misti* was over seventeen thousand feet high, and was visible from almost every part of the city.

Erith thought she would never forget the beautiful splashes of bougainvillaea, the jacaranda trees and geraniums of every hue. She looked around at the well-to-do private properties, and thought Arequipa seemed a very prosperous city.

'Perhaps we should stop for coffee now,' Dom suggested when he could see for himself that she was enjoying herself immensely.

'Must we?' she smiled, not sure if he truly wanted a coffee for himself or if he still had it in mind that she might not be acclimatised to the change in altitude yet.

'We could perhaps compromise,' he smiled, and suggested, 'You might like to see the convent of Santa Catalina—I believe we may also take coffee there.'

'Sounds like a good idea,' she smiled, and liked him very much when his lips twitched.

The convent was in fact, Erith discovered, a miniature town which was set within the city. She and Dom had their coffee first, then set off around the area that dated back to the sixteenth century. She found it quite an experience to walk with Dom from building to building and from street to street, and all within the confines of the convent, which originally served as a boarding school for the daughters of the gentry.

'You enjoyed that too?' he teased her as they left the convent.

'Does it show?' she asked, looking at him with laughing, shining eyes.

'A little,' he smiled, then told her, 'And now it is time for lunch.'

'Already?' she gasped, for although she had walked up an appetite she could hardly believe that it had gone one o'clock.

He took her to a smart restaurant which was a little way off a street which she noted in passing was named Jerusalem Street.

She had rather got into the habit that morning of absorbing everything and anything, and observed then the red plush velvet of the chairs and the red carpet as she and Dom went through to the rear and more secluded part of the restaurant. The walls, she noted, as a waiter swiftly arrived at their table with a menu, were of light wood panelling, and it was all very harmonious.

Which, she felt, went well with her mood. For she and Dom had been in each other's company for some hours now—and not a note of disharmony or discord had once been struck.

'Are you going to choose for yourself, or would you like some help?' he asked her, seeming to know as she opened the menu that she had a tendency to want to try anything new in the culinary line.

'Providing you'll stop me if it seems I'm going to order kippers braised in a marmalade sauce, I'll do it myself,' she grinned.

The outcome of her order of *arroz con camarones* was that she was served with a tasty dish of freshwater shrimps and rice, served with beans and carrots.

'How is it?' asked Dom, a hidden smile looking as though it was wanting to get through.

'Perfectly delicious,' she told him, and when he did smile briefly before he looked away she realised that he knew she would have said her meal was delicious even had it been quite foul.

The service in the restaurant was unhurried, and with Dom an immaculate host, conversing with her in a friendly manner and seeming most interested in anything she had to say, the time simply flew.

Indeed, so well did they seem to be getting along that Erith had forgotten entirely that she had much bigger worries to occupy her mind than what to have for sweet. She decided on a pancake, and had just finished the last tasty mouthful when, as she touched her left hand to her plate, she suddenly caught sight of her watch.

'It's four o'clock!' she exclaimed disbelievingly.

'You haven't noticed the time passing?' Dom asked her, his grey eyes pinning her green ones.

Erith searched for some light remark, then discovered that she couldn't be other than honest with him. 'I've had a super time,' she told him, and was glad she had when, with a warm look entering those eyes that held hers, he smiled.

'Good,' was all he said, and not long afterwards, even though none of the restaurant staff seemed to be anxious that they should be on their way, he settled the bill and they left.

Outside the restaurant, as it was fairly obvious that she was a visitor to Peru, Erith accepted, she was plagued by money-changers who swarmed around like bees, wanting to exchange currency or traveller's cheques for *intis*.

'Is it legal?' she asked Dom when she could see for herself that the money-changers were doing their trade openly and in full view of the banks.

She never did get to hear his reply, but realised that he did not approve of her trying to change a traveller's cheque in the street when, with a curt word or two to one persistent dealer who then melted into the background, Dom flagged down a taxi.

For all his curt tone with the man, though, his good humour was still intact when, back at their hotel, he collected their room keys and went up in the lift with her. 'I'll call for you at eight-thirty,' he told her pleasantly as he opened up the door to her room and stood back.

'I'll—er—be ready,' was all, in a most ridiculously shy moment, that she could think to say.

Idiot! she scolded herself as she wondered what in creation had come over her. She had been with the man for the last seven or eight hours, for goodness' sake, and as far as she could remember had not suffered a single moment of shyness in all that time!

Removing her shoes, she lay on top of her bed, realising that as they had only just finished lunch neither of them would feel like eating again before eight-thirty.

Her glance strayed up to the ceiling, but she saw nothing—only Dom de Zarmoza and his pleasant and interested expression when over lunch she had related one or two happenings in England that connected with any matter he had to comment on.

She thought he was far more interesting than herself, though, and relived again how her questions on his boat business had seen him reveal that he had a yard for building boats in a place called Chimbote, which was much to the north of his hacienda at Jahara.

Jahara, lovely Jahara, her thoughts ran on. Chimbote must be miles and miles away from Jahara, but Jahara was where his roots were. Was it any wonder that, no matter what difficulties there might be in running a business so far away from where he lived, he had not sold up and bought a hacienda near to his boat business? If she owned a part of Jahara, she personally would never voluntarily give it up, she felt certain.

How long Erith lay on her bed with thoughts of beautiful Jahara floating through her mind, she had no idea. But suddenly she discovered that her thoughts had drifted to her actually and physically wanting to be back in that lovely place—and she sat up with a start. Good heavens, what in the world was wrong with her! She was never going to see Jahara again, for goodness' sake!

Really, she scolded silently, she had better things to do than to lie there daydreaming. She was here not to daydream but to find Audra ... At that precise moment, worries which astonishingly had been nowhere in her head for many hours suddenly stampeded in.

By eight twenty-five that evening Erith had been through wave after wave of guilt that she'd been out enjoying—yes, enjoying—herself, while her father and Jean were still waiting anxiously to hear from her. At one point so great did her guilt become that she almost rang Dom's room to see if he had any news yet. But for another absolutely ridiculous moment of shyness when her hand reached the phone, she might well have contacted him. Then she told herself that *he* was bound to contact *her* the moment he had any news. And in any event, she would be seeing him again at half-past eight.

It was a few seconds after eight-thirty when the knock she had been waiting for sounded on her door. Suddenly she discovered that inwardly she felt nowhere near as cool and as composed as she wanted to feel. But, pinning her hopes that her outward appearance did not give away the most peculiar and sudden nervousness which, for no reason, she was all at once feeling, she went and opened the door.

Dom had changed into the same lightweight suit he had worn last night. With a fresh white shirt and a different silk tie, she again thought he looked terrific.

'Hello,' she greeted him, and, ashamed that her voice was suddenly husky, she was glad when he took her door key from her and secured her door. *'Gracias,'* she forced a light note as he handed her back her key.

She saw his mouth pull upwards at the corners, then felt one of his hands on her elbow as he escorted her to the lifts. Her heart began behaving peculiarly again, and it wasn't until they were seated in the hotel's dining-room that she remembered that she hadn't asked him what had been uppermost in her mind to ask him before he had knocked on her door. It was then that she decided that, since nothing was going to change while they had dinner, perhaps it would be more polite to leave it to him to acquaint her with what news he had received on the subject of her stepsister and his nephew.

They were ten minutes into their meal, though, when Erith began to wonder about that decision. He can't possibly have forgotten about Audra and Filipo, can he? she wondered when he had talked easily on several subjects—but not that one.

'Is your steak to your liking?' he questioned when she seemed to be more toying with her meal than eating it.

'Just right,' she replied, realising that good manners, if nothing else, decreed that she pull herself together.

With good manners winning the day, Erith finished her main course. But when the ice cream she had ordered for sweet arrived, and Dom, while conversing comfortably on any matter under the sun, did not say a word on the one issue in particular which she wanted to hear about, she realised she was going to have to bring the subject up herself.

'Were there any messages for you, by the way?' she asked as if she had only just thought about it.

'Messages?' he queried, but as some of the warmth went from his eyes Erith just knew that he was fully aware of what lay behind her question—and for some reason resented her asking it.

But whether he thought she should wait until he chose to tell her anything that there was to tell her, she no longer cared. The frosty way he was now looking at her clearly stated that any friendliness which she had imagined between them was over anyway now.

'You said you'd help me find Audra,' she reminded him sharply. 'You said it was about time you took some time off and that——'

'I'm quite well aware of everything I've said,' he cut her off curtly, any sign of the pleasant companion he had been all day totally gone as he stared at her arctically.

'Then you'll be aware that I'm anxious to hear what replies you've had in answer to your enquiries regarding my stepsister's whereabouts!' Erith said snappily—and was glared at for her trouble.

'Do you think these enquiries can be completed in two minutes?' he challenged shortly, everything about him arrogant and telling her that he cared not at all for her snappy tone.

Well, tough on him! Erith fumed. And, to show him just how much that bothered her, she put her napkin on the table and, finding just sufficient control to remember her manners, told him stiffly, 'Thank you for your company, *señor*. I'm going to bed.'

They both got to their feet at the same time. But Dom did nothing to detain her, as she half thought was his intention. But, with a slight inclination of his head, his manners every bit as good as hers, it seemed, he bade her curtly, 'Goodnight.

When Erith reached her room she discovered that she had begun to shake from that clash of restrained good manners. With a trembling hand she unlocked her door and let herself in.

Closing her door, she leant against it and let go a long-drawn-out breath. Something was definitely happening to disturb her equilibrium since she had arrived in Peru, she realised. A second or two later she moved away from the door, to realise also that that 'something' was all connected with Domengo de Zarmoza. Why was it that *that man* had the power to upset her so?

CHAPTER SIX

ERITH was still no nearer to discovering why Dom had the power to upset her so when, in low humour, she awakened the following morning. He was different, she'd say that for him—not to say infuriating!

As she completed her ablutions, however, it suddenly became patently clear to her that she could not go on the way she was, living on him—for that was what it amounted to. Take away her air-fare home, and she was as good as broke—and no nearer really to finding Audra. Dom, she recalled, had been quite annoyed last night when he'd demanded if she thought his enquiries could be completed in two minutes.

Which, Erith realised, as she left her room, indicated that more and more days could pass, with her living on him. She went down to the breakfast-room wondering what on earth she could have been thinking of anyway that she had allowed him to be out of pocket on her behalf.

Her host was already at breakfast, she saw, but she was in sombre mood as she joined him. 'Good morning,' she murmured, but, too torn apart by the memory of how worried Jean had been on reading that her daughter had got herself engaged to a man whom they knew nothing about, she barely heard his civil reply.

Absently Erith sipped from a cup of coffee that appeared at her right hand and pondered on the possibility of perhaps being able to find some paid employment that would enable her to stay in Peru until she found Audra.

That thought foundered, though, when it occurred to her that, apart from the fact that she couldn't see there being any great demand for a non-Spanish-speaking secretary hereabouts, she realised that if she did find a job she would have succeeded in tying up her time which would be better used in looking for Audra.

She faced then the fact that, from the outset, she had been idiotic in the extreme to have been carried along by her father and her stepmother's worries about Audra. Erith was oblivious to the pensive expression she wore, and was entirely unaware that the man opposite had his eyes on her as, of course, her thoughts went on, she hadn't known at the outset that her money would be stolen, or that Audra and her fiancé would be travelling the country without deigning to...

'What's troubling you?'

As the harsh-sounding question penetrated, Erith looked up swiftly—straight into the grey, brooding eyes of Domengo de Zarmoza. He knows darn well what's troubling me, she thought crossly, and was instantly irritated that if he didn't know, then he jolly well should.

'I've decided to do what I should have done all along,' she informed him coldly, and did not miss the immediate hostility that came to his expression at her tone.

'And that is?' he clipped.

'What else,' she shrugged, 'but to return to England?'

She had aimed for some of his aloofness. But any aloofness she had found went flying as, to her astonishment, he smartly rounded on her and snarled, 'You can't wait to shake the dust of my country off your feet, can you?'

'It's not that at all!' she exclaimed defensively, remembering at once that he had told her one time that his mother preferred to live in her native France, and realising that he must be very touchy on the subject of anyone seeming not to like Peru. 'In other circumstances I'd love to stay longer and see more of your country,' she found herself confessing honestly. 'But...well,' she added lamely, 'you know how I'm situated.'

If Dom appreciated that, financially embarrassed as she was, she and her pride were having the utmost difficulty, he had nothing he wanted to say about it— 'Humph!' was the kind of grunt she got for an answer.

Erith was aware from the sharp look in his eyes, though, that his mind was at work. But she had more to worry about than what he might be thinking. She was going to hate to go home and confess that, though they could be assured that Audra must be all right—or she wouldn't be touring all over Peru, would she?—she hadn't actually spoken to her, or for that matter so much as seen her.

She was in the middle of feeling most despondent at the thought that she had fallen down on the job she had come to do, when once more her host broke through her train of thought.

'It seems to me that, since we've come away from my home and my work, we might as well take advantage of it,' he remarked, his tone bland all at once.

'We?' Erith questioned, her attention all his—even if she was more than a little puzzled to know what he could be talking about.

'It's time I had a holiday,' he announced.

Blinking, Erith could only stare at him uncomprehendingly. Then she remembered his 'we'. 'Where,' she questioned warily, suspicion lurking, 'do I come into this?'

'If you can find it in you to relax, Erith,' he replied smoothly, 'you might find you enjoy it.'

'Enjoy what?' she bit sharply, her suspicion no longer in hiding—and clearly noted by him.

'Do please raise your mind above such things which you've assured me you know nothing of,' he drawled drolly, a mocking look she hadn't expected suddenly appearing in his grey eyes.

'I...' she began to erupt, as a warm pink started to colour her skin.

But she didn't get any further, because all at once his smile broke free, and with a charm that was swamping he said, 'I'm merely suggesting that you might enjoy waiting for your stepsister.'

'Waiting?' she picked up the one word.

'Unfortunately, I heard this morning that my nephew and his companion have moved on yet again.'

'They've...!' Erith broke off, seeing then just how unachievable her task had been anyway.

'There's a lot to see in Peru,' Dom told her, going on. 'I've heard little further except the confirmation that a Señorita Billington is definitely touring the country with Filipo.' He paused, then added, 'Altogether, it makes it seem to me that we could spend many weeks in chasing around trying to catch them.'

'Weeks!' Erith exclaimed, forgetful of her decision to return to England straight away.

'Weeks,' he said apologetically, 'which I just cannot spare.'

'Of course not,' she agreed warmly, in full realisation that he'd been fairly marvellous to have left his work and got involved this far—especially when one remembered that he seemed to have no time for Audra.

'Which is why,' he went on evenly, 'I propose, instead of charging blindly in, wildly trying to catch up with them, that we—you and I—proceed to a place where, if I know my nephew, he's bound to take his—er—love.

A place,' he ended, 'where, instead of being the chasers, we will wait for your stepsister and Filipo to come to us.'

Erith's lovely eyes were large in her face as she stared at Dom. His calculations were little short of brilliant, she realised, and were the obvious answer—she couldn't fault them, anyhow. To her mind it would certainly be easier to be somewhere in advance of them rather than to wait for information and to hare after them only to miss them again.

'Where is this place?' she questioned. 'This place that you're sure Filipo will take Audra?'

'Lake Titicaca,' Dom replied unhesitatingly.

'Lake Titicaca!'

He nodded. 'I'm sure we won't have to wait very long,' he told her.

From having decided not too many minutes ago that she would see about the possibility of getting a flight home to England that day, Erith suddenly discovered that she was wavering. She had gleaned from somewhere that Lake Titicaca was the highest navigable lake in the world, but she was thinking of other things, of her and Dom getting to the Lake before...when suddenly her thoughts broke off—superseded by another thought—a snag, in fact.

'But how do you know that they haven't already visited Lake Titicaca?' she questioned hurriedly. 'They could——'

'They haven't,' he interrupted her. 'There's a hotel there that Filipo particularly cares for—it's unthinkable that he'd use any other. I put through a phone call yesterday—he hasn't been there in six months.'

'Oh,' Erith murmured, and was silent for a few seconds. Then, 'And you'd go with me to Lake Titicaca to wait—as part of your holiday?'

His answer was to make to leave the table. 'It's settled, then,' he commented, clearly a man not to drag his feet.

'Just a minute,' Erith stopped him. He looked across at her and was plainly waiting to hear what else she had to say. 'It's settled—on one condition,' she told him firmly.

She saw at once that, suddenly all proud Peruvian, Dom did not care much for her putting conditions on anything. But, after a lengthy pause during which he eyed her steadily, 'Well?' he asked, and all at once Erith started to feel a trifle uncomfortable.

'I know I'm a bit short of funds right now,' she understated awkwardly—though she went on firmly, 'But I'll only come with you on condition that you allow me to forward you the money for my hotel accommodation when I'm back in England.'

She was right about him not liking her placing conditions on anything. That was underlined for her immediately she saw the arrogant look that came to him. 'First of all you have to return to England,' he documented coldly. 'Then, if I'm not mistaken, you'll have to find employment from which you can earn sufficient to reimburse me.'

'I've every intention of doing that,' she got in tartly, but, as if she had not spoken—and not liking her very much at all, it was plain—he was going on.

'Be assured, *señorita*, that when we get to Lake Titicaca you will have your own room at the hotel.' With that, he got up and left her.

Grief, Erith thought, and didn't need to think about it too deeply to know that she had offended him. Quite obviously he had misinterpreted what she had been saying and thought she was saying she didn't trust him. True, she had been suspicious of him earlier—but he had mockingly allayed any fears she might have nursed, and her trust in him had been total when he'd outlined his plan for them to get to Lake Titicaca before Audra and Filipo.

Erith sighed as she left the breakfast-table. He was such a complex man! Or was it she who was the complex one? It seemed then that she was forever angry with him one minute, and the next, like now, feeling conscience-stricken that she had unwittingly offended him. Something about Peru, she thought not for the first time as she headed out of the dining-room, was certainly making a nonsense out of her normally non-fluctuating temperament.

She wasn't quite sure when exactly she had expected that she might see Dom again. Indeed, from the way he had walked out on her about ten minutes ago, it would not have been too much of a surprise if he had looked straight through her and cut her dead the next time she saw him.

But no, he was coming away from the reception desk as she went to pass through the lobby, and he came over to her. 'We're booked on the ten-thirty flight to Juliaca,' he informed her without preamble, and commanded. 'Have your luggage packed and brought down in half an hour.'

On that instant of being bossed about by him, any lingering feeling of being conscience-stricken about offending him rapidly disappeared. She had never even heard of a place called Juliaca, but, by the look of it, she was being ordered to get her skates on.

'Yes, sir!' she snapped in a voice she was sure he but no one else would hear.

She was up in her room, having cooled down slightly, when she recalled that he had looked about to break into a grin at her snappy retort as she'd abruptly turned from him. Damn him, she thought, she didn't want to amuse

the wretched man. Oh, how she wished she were packing
to go home!

Strangely then, Erith paused, and it was almost as if
there was another part of her that was questioning—did
she really want to go home? Why she should then, at
that precise moment, think of Dom's hacienda, and of
beautiful Jahara, she had no idea. 'This place!' she
scorned out loud, and rushed around to pack, not
wanting to be the one to cause them to miss their flight.

In the event, they arrived at Arequipa airport with
time to spare before the DC8 took off. Time in which
Erith realised she could apologise to Dom, if she had a
mind to, for unintentionally offending him earlier.

For quite some minutes she fought a small battle with
the opposing side of her that wondered why she should
apologise! But, remembering his proud honour, not to
mention the fact that he'd spoken barely two words to
her since she, with her luggage, had joined him back in
the hotel, she suddenly knew she didn't want to fight
with him.

They were seated next to each other waiting for their
flight to be called when she suddenly said his name.
'Dom.' When aloof grey eyes looked down into hers,
though, she began to wish she had left him alone with
his own thoughts. But, since he wasn't saying anything
at all but waiting, unsmiling, for her to continue, 'I just
wanted to say,' was forced from her, 'that I meant what
I said about wanting to repay you for any expense you've
been put to on my account, and,' she added quickly when
she could see his eyes start to frost over, 'to let you know
that I—trust you, utterly and completely.'

Looking into his grey eyes, she thought some of the
frost had melted, but he did not thank her for letting
him know that he had no cause to be offended. Nor, as
they boarded the plane, was his manner any warmer.

They had been airborne about seven minutes when a stewardess served small plastic beakers of *chicha morada*, a non-alcoholic drink made from purple corn. Before Erith could take a sip, though, the plane started to be buffeted about and she was sure her purple drink was going to spill all over her.

Then Dom was ordering her quite pleasantly, 'Fasten your seatbelt, Erith.' But, before she could start to wonder how she could do that while at the same time hanging like grim death on to her drink, he solved the problem by calmly taking the beaker from her hands and downing the contents in one go.

In no time the plastic beaker was deposited in the net pouch secured to the back of the seat in front and—all before she had finished the task he had set her—Dom was turning his attention to her seatbelt.

Why she should feel such a warm glow from his actions, why she should discover that she liked this feeling of being—protected by him, she couldn't have said, for it was a feeling she had never experienced before. All she knew for sure, though, was that she was starting to feel good inside.

That feeling lasted throughout that short and very bumpy flight. It had been announced that the flight would take thirty minutes, but Erith calculated that they must have had a tremendous tail wind when after only twenty minutes their plane safely touched down at Juliaca airport. Oddly, when she was not one hundred percent keen on flying, she had not, since Dom had helped her with her seatbelt, been a bit worried on what at one time she would have called something of a hairy flight.

They left the airport building and Dom escorted her to where he had a hire car waiting. Lake Titicaca was quite some way away from the airport, it seemed. Dom drove effortlessly, and well, and she thought as she

looked around at the *altiplano*, the high plain country
that went on for mile after mile, that he seemed to have
recovered his good humour.

They had been travelling for about an hour when he
slowed down and then stopped the car. 'Would you like
to see the purple corn growing?' he asked.

'The purple corn of the *chicha morada* of which I
nearly had a drink?' she asked saucily.

'I'll see you have another one,' he replied, and to warm
her heart he grinned.

They did not have more than across the road to walk
to see the unfenced acres of purply-pink corn. Some of
the corn had been cut, but there was more that would
shortly be ready to be harvested.

'You can almost hear it growing, it's so peaceful,' Erith
whispered on a note of wonder, standing on that high
plain and feeling as if she was standing on top of the
world.

Switching her gaze away from the harvest, she all at
once found that she was looking up into a pair of grey
eyes that stared down, and suddenly, as for ageless
moments Dom just looked and warmly looked at her,
she felt barely able to breathe. Breathlessly, she had the
oddest feeling that he wanted to touch her—and was
fighting it! And then, at that same moment of her staring
up at him, some never-before-known emotion seemed to
come and take charge of her, and Erith was taken by
the most overwhelming feeling that she wanted to be
touched by him. And all she knew just then was that she
would raise no objection, whatever he chose to do.

Then, abruptly, Dom had turned and found the wide
channels between the rows of corn of particular interest—
and the moment was gone.

Erith was glad to go back to the car where she could
give herself a little talking to—while at the same time

not blame herself entirely. For hadn't she observed before that there was something about this land of Peru that seemed to have her acting and feeling entirely beyond any previous experience?

She had got herself somewhere back together again and had realised that her imagination had a lot to answer for—as if Dom had wanted to touch her, indeed!—when, his voice even and pleasant, and certainly in no way emotionally moved, he remarked, 'We're quite close to some tombs that have been described by at least one knowledgeable person as being the most remarkable ancient monuments in the whole of Peru—would you like to take a look while you're here?'

'Very much,' she replied, and felt quite excited when he parked the car.

'I'm afraid we've something of an upward climb,' he told her as they began their ascent over the grassy path. 'You're feeling all right?' he questioned.

'Great!' she smiled, but somehow discovered that she didn't seem to have very much energy. 'What's this place called?' she asked as she stopped, ostensibly to take in the view.

'Sillustani,' he replied, and as they resumed their slow climb, he told her that Sillustani was the burial-ground of the ancient chiefs of Hatúncolla.

The *chullpas*, or pre-Columbian funeral towers, and the fact that so much labour must have gone into building them, was quite astonishing, to Erith—but she was suddenly beginning to realise that she was not feeling quite at her best.

For some idiotic reason, though, it became a matter of principle—or perhaps pride, she was feeling a little too peculiar to know which—not to let Dom know. So, casually, she would walk a few steps, pause as though

taken by the view, when in actual fact she was catching
her breath before she walked on to repeat the process.

By this method she eventually made it from one side
of the hill summit to the other. It was from there, to her
delight, that she most unexpectedly saw spread out below
a large and beautiful lake.

'Is it Lake Titicaca?' she asked Dom, who had been
interested in funeral chimneys, but who came over to
join her.

'Titicaca is a bit bigger, I think, and goes on into
Bolivia,' he smiled. 'This is Lake Umayo.'

Ten minutes later, having enjoyed the scenery, they
began their way back down. By then Erith, who was
feeling quite unwell, was dreading having to move again
at all. But she found the going down far easier than the
climb up had been.

'Thank you, I enjoyed that,' she told Dom once they
were back in the car, and conversed with him easily
enough until they reached their hotel.

It was as he was signing them into the hotel, though,
that she began to feel sick. At one stage she had the
most frightening feeling that she was going to have to
start screaming for the ladies' room. But the feeling
passed, and in the next minute Dom had taken charge
of their room keys and, while leaving their luggage for
the porter to attend to, was escorting her to the lift.

They had reached the floor their rooms were on and
Dom had inserted a key into one of the doors when her
feeling of wanting to be ill returned—with a vengeance.

There was no hope of her battling to suppress it this
time. 'Quick!' she cried in alarm. 'I'm going to be sick!'
She had a hasty vision of Dom's startled look first at
the urgency in her voice, then at what she'd said. And
then maybe because as he looked into her face her

normally pale skin took on a green tinge that went well with her eyes, he moved.

That all happened in about a split second. In the next split second one of his Spanish epithets had hit her ears, then the door was open and with a strong arm about her he had swiftly taken her into the bathroom.

To her undying gratitude, she was not sick. 'It's—gone off!' she gasped, still feeling dreadful, but glad to find she no longer felt like making an exhibition of herself in front of him.

'How long have you been feeling ill?' he asked shortly.

'I'm sorry,' she apologised, feeling miserable, unhappy, and above all, aware that he wasn't thrilled.

Another epithet escaped him, then a brief moment of heaven was hers as he pulled her close so she could rest her head against his chest. 'Idiot child,' he told her gently. 'I'm angry with me, not you.'

'Why?' she asked, feeling her legs were about to buckle.

'I should have noticed you were suffering.'

'No, you shouldn't,' she began to contradict him. 'I didn't want you to...' She broke off, and clutched on to him. 'I want to go to bed,' she told him.

She felt she had never liked him more when, swinging her up in his arms, he teased, 'Of all the times to issue such an invitation!'

She put an arm around his neck as he carried her from the bathroom, and snuggled up to him. 'I'm so cold,' she told him.

'I know,' he said gently, as he lowered her to the bed and took off her shoes.

'What's the matter with me?' she asked as she searched the covers for an opening so she could get into bed.

'*Soroche*—mountain sickness—it's nothing to worry about, you'll be over it in a couple of days,' he assured her. 'We're more than four thousand feet higher up here than we were in Arequipa. Some people get it, some don't,' he assured her soothingly, and while Erith who was by then under the covers was tiredly thinking that without a doubt Dom would be one of those who didn't get it, he enquired kindly, 'Don't you think you might feel better if you got undressed?'

'No,' she replied groggily, and closed her eyes.

She was vaguely aware of noises in the room as the porter came in with the the luggage, and gathered from the length of conversation which Dom had with him that he was instructing him to take his case to his room. Then, not many minutes afterwards, she could swear, someone from room service had come and gone and Dom was instructing, 'Sit up and drink this, Erith.'

'What is it?' she asked, and because he was Dom and she liked him, she opened her eyes and struggled to sit up.

'*Coca* tea,' he replied, and heaven was hers again when he went behind her and held her against him while she sipped of the hot liquid that tasted of nothing in particular. 'It's the accepted remedy for altitude sickness,' he continued to talk to her.

'I'll take your word for it,' she mumbled.

'Will you also take my word for it that you'll feel better if you get into your nightclothes?'

'I don't think I've got that much energy,' she told him, and felt confused when, her tea finished, he propped her against her pillows and passed her her shoulder-bag.

'I'll need your case keys,' he told her.

It seemed easier to find them for him than argue. She did argue, though, when Dom, having unlocked her case and extracted her nightdress, approached the bed and— since she had told him she didn't have any energy—

seemed ready to personally divest her of her daytime clothes.

'It's only afternoon!' She pushed his hands away as, dropping her nightdress on the bed, he reached towards the buttons of her shirt.

It was then that he sat down on her bed and took a gentle hold of her hands. Then quietly, 'Erith, my dear,' he said softly, 'I know, and believe, that no man has ever taken such liberties with you. But you're ill and will be far more comfortable in your bed dressed other than you are.' And when Erith stared at him from large unhappy eyes, 'What happened to ''I trust you utterly and completely''?' he teased.

'Oh, Dom!' she cried, so mournfully that suddenly he moved closer and soothingly cradled her in his arms. And, just as suddenly, peace washed over her. She felt comforted in his arms, contented even. How that was possible when at the same time she felt so absolutely exhausted she had no idea, but that was how she felt. For an age he cradled her to him just like that, and then she found some strength from somewhere. 'I'm all right now,' she told him, and raised her head.

'Sure?' he queried softly.

'Sure,' she smiled, and knew even more comfort when, tenderly, he laid his lips against hers.

He was totally businesslike, however, as he murmured, 'Let's have the top layer, anyhow,' and, dropping her nightdress over her head and then keeping his eyes steady on her face, he undid the buttons on her shirt. Once his hand brushed against her breast, but she knew it was unintentional, and when her shirt was gone, and she had slipped her arms into the armholes of her nightdress, he had undone the waistband of her trousers and, moving to the end of the bed, had under cover of the bedclothes pulled them from her. And Erith was exhausted. 'Rest now,' he instructed, but she didn't need any telling.

It was still daylight outside when he awakened her and introduced a doctor she had never heard enter the room. 'I don't need a doctor!' she stated the first thing to come into her head.

'I'm sure you don't,' Dom quietened her calmly. 'But if you're in need of any medication, the doctor here is just the person to prescribe it for you.'

It did not take long for the doctor to confirm that she had an attack of mountain sickness. 'You should be well in a day or two,' he told her in quite good English while, switching to Spanish, he handed Dom a phial of tablets. 'If not, it may be necessary for you to descend to a lower altitude.'

'Thank you,' she said politely, and would have loved to have gone back to sleep.

'Feeling hungry?' asked Dom, coming back into the room after seeing the doctor out.

'Not at all,' she replied, then suddenly had the most tremendous attack of conscience for her thought-lessness. 'Oh!' she cried in anguish. 'Have you been here all the time?'

'I assure you, Erith, that I have been merely watching you while waiting for the doctor to arrive,' Dom informed her, a shade stiffly, she thought.

'I didn't mean I objected,' she jumped in quickly, to set matters straight. 'I meant, if you've been here all this while, that you must be starving. You've had no lunch,' she went on hurriedly, her breathing starting to get laboured, 'and it—must be nearly—time for dinner!'

'Hush, now!' Dom came and sat on the twin bed next to hers, and taking a gentle hold of her hand, 'You must concentrate on conserving your energy and not worrying about me or anything else. I won't starve,' he assured her, and went on, 'Now, do you think you could manage some soup?'

After that, Erith drifted in and out of sleep. She had been glad, when her soup arrived, to see that he had ordered a meal for himself. And she was surprised, and pleased, to find that she managed to down most of the hot soup, though more because she thought she should than because it was what she wanted. When Dom finished his meal she told him she would be perfectly all right if he wanted to leave.

'I'll stay awhile,' he replied easily, giving her an all-assessing look. She slept, then woke, and it had gone midnight when, first having been assured that she needed nothing, Dom went to his own room.

Erith spent a disturbed night. At first, though, she could think of nothing but Dom and his kindness. As the early hours crept on, however, and she began to relate his goodness in coming with her this far to wait for Audra and Filipo to the reason she had come to Peru, her thoughts suddenly turned into nightmare ones. And all at once she was starting to panic that she had been in Peru for so long, and yet, though she knew that her father and Jean must be watching every post, she had not so much as sent them a postcard!

There were good reasons for that, of course, she tried to tell herself as she wondered if anxiety attacks were all part and parcel of the sudden and debilitating effects of mountain sickness. Whether it was or whether it wasn't, though, she was overwhelmingly glad to have company when, at a few minutes before six, Dom let himself into her room with the key he must have taken with him.

She smiled at him, liking the freshly showered and shaven look of him. 'How are you?' he asked, coming over to the bed and giving her that same all-assessing scrutiny he had given her on leaving.

Oh, Dom, she thought, and felt quite weepy at his kindness, for he could have had very little sleep. 'Much better,' she lied, and saw at once from his sceptical look that here was one man it wasn't easy to fool.

'You didn't sleep well either, did you?' he questioned severely, and while, bearing in mind that he probably knew that she felt exhausted enough to sleep the clock round, she wondered how he knew she had had such a dreadful night, 'You saw me eat a man-size meal,' he suddenly changed serious tack to tease, 'so what else is worrying you, little one?'

His charm floored her. 'Oh, Dom,' she said softly, and found she was confessing , 'It's—er—a bit of a—problem to me that I haven't written to my father and stepmother yet. They'll be waiting for me to make contact, but——'

'Consider the problem solved,' Dom cut her off in the nicest possible way. And while Erith stared at him, seeking to know how the problem could possibly be solved, he went on easily, 'There aren't any international telephone wires here, but if you'll let me have their address, I'll send a cable.'

'A cable!' Open-mouthed, Erith stared at him. He made it all sound so simple. Her brain, however, soon thought of a hitch. 'But what can I possibly tell them?' she asked, and discovered that he had a simple answer to that too.

'How about, "Audra well and happy, love, Erith"?' he supplied.

Erith stared solemnly into his steady eyes. 'It wouldn't be lying, would it?' she said seriously.

'According to my information,' Dom replied quietly, 'your stepsister has everything she's set her heart on.'

Suddenly the sun came out for Erith, and, bearing in mind that she instinctively knew she would not be rushing around anywhere for a few days, all seemed very much all right with her world.

'Will you send that cable for me?' she asked him with a smile.

His glance strayed to the sweet curve of her mouth, but although she knew he was teasing, there was no answering smile when, 'For you, Erith,' he replied, 'anything.'

CHAPTER SEVEN

IT SEEMED incredible that she'd been at Lake Titicaca for going on four days now, Erith mused when she awakened on Sunday morning. She got out of bed and pattered to the bathroom, took a shower, and was overwhelmingly relieved that the feeling of exhaustion that had been there when she had finished showering yesterday was nowhere about. Gone too was the tingling sensation in her fingertips, nor was she breathless, she noticed as she returned to her bedroom.

She had, in fact, she realised as she sat down and brushed her long hair, started to feel stronger once her appetite had returned, and had known then that it would not be necessary, as the doctor had suggested, for her to descend to a lower altitude.

She owned that she had Dom to thank for her wellbeing. Wellbeing in more ways than one, she accepted. For as well as seeing to it that she used up as little energy as possible in these days of her getting acclimatised, he, by virtue of the fact of sending that cable to England, had eased her mental anxieties a tremendous amount. In fact, she realised, since she had been at Lake Titicaca, the importance of her quest seemed to be getting dimmer and dimmer in her mind all the time.

Nor did she feel any urgency about it then, for her thoughts had winged to Dom again, and as a small frown puckered her brow the hairbrush in her hands was suddenly motionless. Something, she could not pinpoint what, had altered. She thought, was sure, that it stemmed from him, because, while watching like a hawk that she

116

didn't do anything in any way strenuous, at the same time he seemed to have changed somehow.

She had no idea quite how he had changed. He was kind and considerate still, but... Well, he no longer teased her, for one thing, she drew out of the hat, and he seemed to be—well, brooding about something—sort of.

Starting to feel impatient with herself, yet sure she was not imagining that there was a change in him somewhere, Erith left her seat and went over to the window to stare and then stare some more at the great expanse of Lake Titicaca spread out below.

In no time, however, her thoughts were back to Dom. Why would he be brooding, for goodness' sake? He was on holiday, wasn't he? Her spirits plummeted as she faced the fact that yes, he was on holiday, but he would without a doubt by far have preferred to have chosen his holiday companion rather than have the one he had thrust upon him.

With such thoughts predominating, Erith was not in her sunniest mood when, shortly before eight, Dom came and knocked on her door. 'Ready for breakfast?' he enquired, looking intently down into her face as though judging the state of her health.

'I'll get my bag,' she told him, and ducking back into her room, wondered from the racing of her heart if perhaps she wasn't quite so acclimatised as she thought.

'You're very quiet!' he commented when, five minutes into breakfast, she had said barely a word. And, when she had no answer to make, 'Are you feeling as well as you look?' he queried sharply.

'I'm fine,' she told him, a shade sharply herself, she had to admit. 'Thank you,' she added, because whatever ailed him—or her either, for that matter—good manners cost nothing.

'You're bored!' he announced, and added, 'Up until now you haven't been fit enough to do any exploring. I suggest this morning that we——'

'No!' she interrupted him hurriedly, and at his arrogant look, 'It's—it's not fair to you,' she added quickly.

'What isn't?' he wanted to know.

'You're here on holiday. You didn't choose to have me as your companion,' she went on to explain some of her earlier thoughts. 'It's you who must be bored silly to——'

'My dear Erith,' Dom cut in, his voice suddenly taking on that lovely teasing note which only then did she realise how sorely she had missed it, 'do shut up.'

'But . . .' she wanted to protest still, though, with her heart feeling suddenly so much lighter than it had, her protest was not as strong as it might have been.

Her heart was lighter still when, not waiting, he said solemnly, the most delicious light twinkling in his eyes, 'Do you think, *señorita*, that were I bored by you, or did not want your company, I should suggest you might care to accompany me on a visit to the floating islands this morning?'

'No. . . I . . . Floating islands?' she queried.

'I thought that would arouse your interest,' he grinned. Erith smiled.

An hour later, Dom led her down a steep path to the water's edge where, plainly by prior arrangement, a man stood overseeing a small motorised boat. Dom passed a few words with the man and handed him a bundle of notes, then turned to hand her into the boat.

At first Erith thought the man was coming with them, but no sooner had Dom started up the dainty-sounding engine of the small craft than it became apparent that it would be just her and the tall Peruvian. From then, and for the next few hours, Erith spent some of what she thought were the most enraptured moments of her life.

The floating islands were in actual fact reed structures which sometimes drifted about the lake or were anchored by long tap-roots. The Uros Indians, inhabitants of the islands, were said to be the first Indians to migrate to South America. Dom filled in more of her education as they stepped ashore on one of the islands on to a floor made of totora reeds.

'The pure-bred Uro have disappeared from this region now, I believe,' he told her as, their boat secured, he aided her from the small jetty to an open-air area where small bowler-hatted women were busy at work making colourful handicrafts for sale.

'Aren't these people Uros Indians?' Erith queried, stopping when with a shy smile and hand signs one of the sturdily built women invited her to inspect a wall hanging she was embroidering.

'They're descendants of the Uro, but have a mixture of Aymara in their blood,' Dom enlightened her, and it was in that language, Aymara, that he spoke to a group of men who were busily engaged in what looked to Erith remarkably like a one-sided tug-o'-war exercise.

'What are they doing?' she looked up at him to enquire.

For long, long seconds Dom looked down at her without reply, and suddenly she felt tensed up and breathless. Oddly, she had the strangest notion that he was about to kiss her. She was barely breathing as, feeling unable to move a muscle, she just continued to look at him—and then he looked away.

'It seems that more room and accommodation is required now that a couple of young members of the community are about to marry,' Dom answered, plainly not having the smallest inclination to kiss her. And, to show just how totally wrong she was, proving that the idea of kissing her had never entered his head, his voice easy and relaxed, he went on, 'What's happening now is that another piece of totorales is being heaved into position in order to extend the size of this island.'

'Good heavens!' Erith murmured, as she tried with all she had to recover and wonder that her imagination could have played her so false.

They left that island with Dom making a donation at the reed-built schoolhouse, and progressed to another island where Erith recovered her equilibrium and found everything about her peaceful and tranquil once more.

The main industry on that particular island seemed to be fishing, and she watched fascinated as fish caught earlier were laid out in neat rows while waiting for a stone to be hot enough for cooking. The cooked fish, she learned, were later taken to market.

'That was absolutely out of this world,' she told Dom when some while later they left that island with its reed huts and friendly people, and he steered their light-engined boat through tall-growing reeds.

'You enjoyed it?' he enquired, and at the good-humoured look of him Erith was prepared to believe that—with her imagination playing up the way it was—she had imagined that he had been in any way different over the last couple of days.

Perhaps it wasn't even him, but her, and that wretched mountain sickness was the cause. 'Tremendously,' she replied honestly, her eyes ashine from the pleasure of it all. She turned in her seat beside him and looked back the way they had come. 'It's so peaceful, so tranquil,' she shared with him her earlier thoughts.

'Heavenly, in fact,' he teased, and smiled, and Erith knew, right at that moment—without knowing what exactly—that there was something special about this man.

'I don't care if you do think I'm going over the top,' she told him, 'this is my first visit to Lake Titicaca and...' she faltered as a dart of sudden disconsolation hit her '...and probably my last,' she went on quietly.

Silence reigned in the boat for a while, then, 'That seems as good a reason as any for prolonging our trip on the water,' Dom said evenly, and at her questioning look, 'How does a waterborne picnic appeal?' he asked.

'Really? Can we?' she questioned, and was at once happy again.

It was all the answer he required as, unhurriedly, with even the motor of the boat sounding quite genteel, he steered on for about another half-hour, then pulled into the reeded shallows and cut the engine.

Erith discovered that she very much liked her picnics with Dom. He must, she realised, have arranged for the food to be prepared during the hour after he'd 'suggested' she might care to visit the floating islands with him.

Conversation between them was easy and desultory as she nibbled on a sandwich and looked on while Dom opened up a bottle of Inca Kola and poured it into a glass before handing it to her. She really felt then, in that peaceful setting, as if she were indeed on holiday with him.

Thoughts of Audra, or of her family back in England, were far from her mind in any event as she ended her meal with a slice of cake and rinsed her fingers in the clear crystal waters of Lake Titicaca.

Out as far as she could see stretched the waters of the lake with mountains forming a backcloth. The clearness of the water was astonishing, and she observed where the blue sky above with its smattering of pure white clouds was mirrored perfectly in the vast waters.

Soon, however, the peace of the scene had a soporific effect, and she was leaning back in the cushions of the bench seat and feeling pleasantly drowsy when she asked the totally unimportant question, 'Are those clouds cumulus or nim...?'

'You're asking *me*?' queried an amused voice by her side, and Erith lost all feeling of drowsiness, as she erupted into laughter and turned to look at Dom.

'Your English is so good, I keep forgetting that it isn't your mother tongue,' she told him, and, as she saw his glance flick to her curving mouth—and rest there for what seemed an age before he dragged his gaze back to her eyes, she was all at once tense again. Suddenly—and she knew she was not imagining it this time—she was sure that Dom not only wanted to kiss her, but that he was going to.

'Dom!' she breathed his name huskily, and to her ears his name on her lips sounded like an invitation.

It was an invitation which he wasted no time in accepting, and in the next moment his long arms were reaching for her. Unafraid, she willingly moved towards him, then his head came down and his lips met hers.

How long that kiss went on, she neither knew nor cared. What she did know was that it was like no kiss she had ever known before. With Dom's arms strong iron bands around her, she felt secure and as if nothing could ever harm her.

'Erith!' he murmured her name when he broke the kiss, and when she smiled gently up at him it was as if he found the curve of her mouth totally irresistible, for he lowered his head and kissed her again.

And suddenly Erith was on a voyage of discovery. She discovered that she found his warm and mobile mouth irresistible too. More, that she wanted more. Eagerly she responded to his kisses. He did not need a second invitation, but pulled her closer up to him. Somehow the narrow confines of the boat seemed to represent no obstacle. Their bodies melded even closer together as

Dom used his body to press her further back against the cushions.

'Dom!' she whispered his name again when tender gentle hands caressed her throat.

Again he kissed her, and her arms wound up and around him and she strained to get even closer to him. She felt one of his hands move caressingly down to capture and mould one of her breasts, and had never experienced before the surge of longing that took her then.

Her grip on his shoulder tightened, and she clutched on to him as his other hand went down to the waistband of her trousers. But it was as his long artistic fingers started to undo the fastenings that she discovered a couple of other things. The one, that for the first time in her life she was in a position with a man where she wanted to deny him nothing. The other discovery was so earth-shattering to her that at just that moment it transcended the desire Dom had aroused in her. For that discovery, unwanted, unbidden, but there just the same, was that she—was in love with him!

'Oh!' she cried, and was in such shock then that she was acting on instinct only as she made a sudden jerky movement, as if to get away, and somehow succeeded in knocking Dom's hands from her.

If he was startled that in the span of a split second she had changed from a clinging, vibrant woman into a woman who now seemed to be desperately wanting to put some space between them, then he covered it very well.

He wasted no time in moving his long length from against her, anyhow, and Erith felt at one and the same time both relieved and anxious. She wanted to apologise, then didn't know what she wanted to apologise for, so she sat tensely, saying nothing but, in stunned silence, staring as if hypnotised at his hands which were now oddly clenched fast round the steering wheel.

For many long seconds they sat just like that, with neither of them saying a word. Erith's head was, by then, all over the place. But while she was striving hard to show a fairly bland front until she could get to be by herself, it suddenly dawned on her that since clearly Dom had desired her, it could perhaps be that he needed some time to get himself under control.

She guessed she was right when suddenly he reached forward and started the quiet outboard motor. 'It might be a good idea if we returned to the hotel,' he said stiffly, at long last breaking the taut silence. Erith could not find a word to say.

The whole of her being came roaringly alive again when, having moored the boat, he turned and took hold of her hands to help her alight. Once she was on *terra firma*, however, Erith, her skin burning from the tingling touch of him, swiftly pulled her hands out of his. She fancied that he uttered one of his Spanish epithets, but she wasn't sure and she wasn't of a mind to look at him to see if she had offended him.

She felt an overwhelming need to be by herself and wanted to hurry up the steep incline back to the hotel. Thoughts that Dom, mindful of her recent altitude sickness, might physically restrain her if she set off at a cracking pace was all the deterrent she needed. She wanted his touch, yet—because of what it could do to her—she felt, confusedly, that he mustn't touch her again. She was never more aware of him, though, as they walked up the path to the hotel.

What he was thinking as inside the hotel he collected their room keys she had no idea, but he offered nothing in the way of conversation. She had fast come to the conclusion that she *had* offended him, not only by snatching her hands from his some minutes ago, but also by responding eagerly to his kisses the way she had—only to suddenly put up a brick wall.

They reached the door of her room and he inserted the key in the lock, opened her door and then handed the key to her. Then, when she had grown fairly certain that he might never speak to her again, he turned and before leaving her suggested, his tone even, 'It might be an idea if you rested this afternoon.'

Damn the *soroche*, she thought once she was alone. But there was no heat in her annoyance that despite his being silently furious with her he was still watchful that she did not overdo things. Which made it most confusing that, if he was so watchful of her, he should have been ready to make love to her out on the lake!

Erith slumped down in a chair and faced the fact that while she supposed she should thank her lucky stars that Dom was gentleman enough, and had control enough, to stop making love to her when it seemed she had demurred, there was little hope that she would be able to get any rest that afternoon.

She might rest physically, she conceded as the minutes started to tick by, but her head was filled with such confusion and mental torment that there seemed no escape.

Having spent some hours with her mind in an uproar, around five o'clock in a desperate desire to concentrate her thoughts on something else, she decided to take a shower.

Fat chance, she thought unhappily as the water cascaded over her slender body. Dom, and the full catastrophe of what she had done, was everywhere. Oh, how *could* she have been so crass as to have fallen in love with him? He had given her no encouragement to do so and would be astounded if he ever found out. Not that he would, she'd take jolly good care about that.

As she had several times previously in the last hours, Erith investigated any faint ray of hope that Dom might

similarly care for her. She found it heartening to believe
from the one or two comments he had let fall that he
must like her, but liking, she knew, as her heartened
feelings again plummeted, was a very long way from
loving. She saw no cause for rejoicing in the fact that
he had obviously felt desire for her out there on the lake.
He was a man, wasn't he? With her meeting him more
than halfway once he had kissed her, she was honest
enough to know that the rest, up to her shattering realisation that she loved him, was fairly inevitable.

Erith was still trying to get away from thoughts of
Dom and how soon, before too long, she must leave his
country and him, as she slipped from the shower and
began to dry herself. But, to show how muddled her head
was, she just then realised that she hadn't taken a change
of underwear into the bathroom with her.

Wrapping the bath towel around her, she swiftly left
the bathroom and was over by a set of drawers and about
to pull one out, when to her alarm the door to her room
was suddenly pushed open.

Her alarm that some intruder had burst into her room
was promptly negated when she at once recognised the
tall grey-eyed man who now stood staring at her.

Hurriedly, as other emotions stormed in and she observed the aggressive way he was looking at her, Erith
made valiant strides to pull herself more together. 'You
might have knocked!' she told him as coolly as she was
able, given that she could feel the bath towel she had
around her—her only covering—start to slip.

'I did!' Dom replied sharply, and, while Erith was realising that as she hadn't heard him knock it would be
second nature to him to test the door-handle, he snarled
suddenly, 'Haven't you the sense to lock your door?'
and as his glance raked over her and her scant attire, he
closed the door, and rapped, 'Just about anybody could
have come in!'

'I . . .' she tried, but had no defence. Not that with so much else on her mind it was any surprise to her that she had forgotten to lock her door. But she felt engulfed just then by a sea of vulnerability, and could find nothing else to say.

Too late, she realised that some of what she must be feeling must be showing in her face, because suddenly all sign of aggressiveness went from Dom, and he had taken a couple of strides nearer to her as he asked quietly, 'Are you all right, Erith?'

Oh, help, she thought, and the fact that the towel she had around her had slipped another inch was the least of her problems as she fought desperately to hide what was in her heart.

'I'm fine!' she replied brightly, but experienced more alarm when he came even closer still and, as though trying to gauge what went on inside of her, looked down into the depths of her large green eyes.

'You're sure?' he queried, and absolutely terrified her when, making her heart beat clamorously, he placed cool hands on her bare shoulders. And, while still looking down into her eyes, he held her steady as with a small movement of his head towards the window and the lake beyond he told her, 'I didn't mean to frighten you—out there.'

Erith's emotions were in such a riot just then that she was paying very little heed to the fact that Dom seemed to be trying to reassure her about something. All she knew for sure was that somehow, she had to hide her innermost feelings.

She strove with all she had to hide her panicking agitation, and was never more pleased that not a sign of panic showed, but her tone sounded lofty, uncaring even, as she replied, 'No problem.'

'No problem!' Dom echoed, but there was that something there in his voice—no longer kind or solicitous—

that warned her he was not terribly thrilled by her lofty manner.

'I've been kissed before,' she attempted, as she made to move round him—it seemed a good idea to head back to the bathroom.

'I'm sure you have,' he clipped, and panicked her wildly as he grated, a hand snaking out to manacle her upper arm, 'But you've never before responded quite like—*this*,' and before she could blink he had pulled her, none too gently, into his arms.

'No!' was about the full extent of any protest she had time to make—then his mouth was over hers.

No, she wanted to protest again, but she couldn't, and in less than seconds, as Dom crushed her to him she was losing any notion of why she should want to protest at all.

She was clinging to him when his kisses gentled, and all fight or any idea of fighting him had left her. She clutched on to him as, his mouth leaving hers, he traced tender kisses from her shoulder and along her throat, until he again claimed her mouth. When he gently hoisted her up in his arms and carried her the few steps to her bed, she had no objection to make.

She thrilled to his touch when he lay down on the mattress with her. The towel that covered her was all anyhow about her now, but as Dom looked deeply into her eyes, her scanty covering bothered her little.

'Erith, my sweet Erith,' he whispered, her name on his lips, the endearment alone sending her into ecstasies,

'Oh, Dom!' she sighed, and gently he kissed her. She felt his fingers caressing her face, her throat, and as his kiss deepened she pressed to get closer to him. She loved him, was in love with him, and as his fingers moved down to caress and capture her naked breast, loving him was all that mattered.

'All right?' he whispered, his voice sounding slightly hoarse to her ears, but whether he was asking was she all right, or if what he was doing to her was all right, she did not know.

But, 'Oh yes!' she breathed rapturously, and as he was able to touch her body she discovered a need in her to touch his.

She extended a shy hand to the buttons of his shirt, and loved him more when he caught hold of her hand, raised it to his lips and then, undoing his shirt himself, shrugged out of it.

'Oh,' she cried softly when moments later he pressed his naked hair-roughened chest to her uncovered bosom.

Time was ageless then as they kissed and caressed. Then a moment or two of shyness unexpectedly inhibited Erith when, vaguely aware that only a small part of the bath towel separated her from complete nudity, Dom gently started to remove it.

'No!' she exclaimed on a small sound of agitation.

'No?' he queried, his eyes steady, understanding, she realised as he looked down into her flushed face.

She swallowed hard, wanting to deny him nothing. 'I'm sorry,' she apologised, and then after a deep breath, 'Yes,' she told him.

'My darling!' he breathed, but instead of taking the towel from her, he brought both hands up to cup her face. Then he tenderly kissed her.

Oh, Dom, I love you so, she wanted to tell him, but could not; she could only show him how much she loved him, by taking hold of a part of the bath towel herself and, giving it a tug, letting it fall to the floor. 'Oh, Dom!' she breathed, and gloried in her nakedness as she raised her arms up and wound them about him, and pressed her body close up against his.

She heard him groan, heard the endearment he breathed in his own tongue, and knew yet more rapture when his hands caressed her and moved freely over her breasts, waist and hips.

'You darling, my brave darling,' he breathed on discovering her total nakedness, and, to cause her colour to flare, he moved her to lie a small way apart from him. Then, unhurriedly, he transferred his ardent gaze from her face and, for the first time, fastened his eyes on the uncovered contours of her silken body. 'You're beautiful!' he breathed softly, as he stretched out a hand to gently stroke in turn the hardened pink peaks of her breasts. One hand was still at her breasts when, easily and entirely without embarrassment, he removed another piece of his clothing. He then turned again to her and with his arms encircling her body he pulled her up against him, their legs intertwining. 'Is it any wonder that I can't keep my hands off you?' he smiled.

Erith felt pretty much the same about him. 'Can't you?' she asked.

'Do I have to?' he replied, and she knew then that if she replied 'No', he would make complete and beautiful love to her.

She opened her mouth to tell him a smiling no, then abruptly, someone knocked hard on her door. For a stunned second she could not believe her hearing. Then the knock came again. And all at once, as swift and hurried memory arrived of how Dom had knocked at her door and on receiving no reply, had walked in, inhibitions, shyness and modesty, which up until then had not been overwhelmingly evident, suddenly awoke and began to make up for lost time.

With a cry of fear in case whoever it was walked in and saw her naked on her bed—and Dom, on the bed with her, nearly naked too—Erith, before Dom could be aware of what was happening, had pushed him away and sprinted for the bathroom. With shaking fingers she rapidly slammed the bolt home.

Suddenly she became aware of the cool tiles beneath her bare feet. Then, as she caught sight of herself in the mirror and saw her much heightened colour—colour which Dom must have observed when he'd been looking at her a few moments earlier—Erith concealed herself in another towel, and collapsed on to the edge of the bath.

She clutched the bath as she heard sounds to indicate that Dom had gone to answer the door. She heard an exchange of voices, then heard the door close, but by then she was shaking so badly that she wanted, with everything that was in her, to race back to Dom, to be held by him and comforted. That then, though, was when it started to penetrate that, whatever else had been between them just now, it had not been *that* sort of comfort.

It was then that she realised that, while Dom had wanted her as she had wanted him—and still did—as far as he was concerned there would have been nothing more to their lovemaking than mutual pleasure.

And that, she faced, had nothing whatsoever to do with what, at the heart of her, she wanted. It dawned on her that she was a mass of contradictions because even while she was acknowledging that she wanted a love in which shared physical pleasure was a part, she was at the same time thinking that surely there had to be a place too in love, to be held, and comforted, without physical desire being paramount?

For long agitated minutes Erith stayed in the bathroom feeling confused, bewildered, but feeling a great need, too, to have Dom understand that never having been in such an intimate situation before, she had been so confused when someone had knocked at the door that she had just bolted for cover.

It was at about that point that she realised that Dom must be waiting for her to emerge from the bathroom, and she found she was half hoping that he would come to the bathroom to get her. She had a feeling that all he'd need to do would be to call her name from the other side of the door and that she would go out to him.

But he did not call her name, and suddenly her straining ears were picking up sounds which told her he had got tired of waiting. She heard the door leading from her room open and close, and was so totally confused by everything that had taken place that day that she could not have said if she was glad or sorry he had gone.

She was still shaking badly when, just in case her ears had played her false, she left her bolthole and, with her heart thumping, stepped into her bedroom. The room was empty. Dom *had* gone. On her bed lay a small parcel of clean laundry which she had put out for washing yesterday. And the only reminder there of the passionate way she had clung to Dom was the bath towel which now lay on the floor at the other side of the bed.

By the time the hands on her watch neared the hour when Dom normally called for her so that they should go down for dinner, Erith had been through a whole gamut of emotions, She had swung from being an in-love woman to one who was hopeful of holding everything back. In particular, the fact that she was in love with him.

Quite how she was going to get across to him that she was *not* in love with him, when from where she viewed it she had, by her heated response, nearly shouted the fact out loud, Erith did not know. At one stage she had been of the opinion that she would go without her dinner that night rather than face him. But that, she soon realised, would be more revealing than anything.

Which was why she was inwardly trembling and outwardly calm as, dressed in the nicest dress she had with her, she waited. It crossed her mind many times that Dom might not call. It was not the first time she had been all responsive in his arms, only to back off when previously she had shown not the slightest sign of being anything but forward, she recalled. Perhaps he had grown so fed up with her vacillating behaviour that it had become too much for even the gentleman in him, and he had decided that she could starve as far as he was concerned before he'd give her a call.

It did not come to that, however, for a few minutes later there came a tap at her door. Instantly her heart started to beat furiously, and as warm colour flared into her face she went towards the door. Before she could open the door, though, Erith just had to take a few seconds in which to try and get herself under some sort of control. When that proved useless, she opened the door.

Dom, tall and straight, stared down at her, his grey eyes kind as they rested on her flushed face. 'Hungry?' he enquired easily, his glance taking in her expression, though there was not an atom of anything about him to suggest he remembered a moment of the passion that had flared between them, or an instant of how, naked, she had lain in his arms.

'Starving,' she told him, and with Dom conversing effortlessly they went down to dinner, and Erith was finding, unbelievably in view of her prior inner torment, that she was feeling much more comfortable with him than she would have thought.

Whether he was deliberately doing all he could to put her at her ease, she could not have said. But, as she began to eat her meal, she realised that it could be partly that, or partly his natural charm, or even partly the fact that she had been worrying unnecessarily anyway. Could it not be that she had taken the scene that afternoon out of all proportion? Could it be that, the happenings of that day showing her far more physically involved with a man than she had ever, *ever* been, everything had gone haywire and gigantic in her mind.

But there was no time then to go further into self-analysis because, their first course out of the way, Dom was charming her with some anecdote about his childhood. She had no idea how they had got on to the subject, but, loving him—even if she was at pains to hide it—she wanted to hear more and yet more about him.

'Your childhood was spent in Peru, of course?' she questioned with a pleasant show of passing interest.

'Mainly,' he replied. 'Though, with my mother living in France, I occasionally spent some time there.'

'Ah,' Erith murmured, and thought she had the answer then to the question of whether his mother had left Peru *before* his father had died.

'What does the "Ah" signify?' Dom asked her, and, because there was a quirky sort of smile at the corners of his mouth which she liked very much, Erith smiled back.

'Your parents were divorced?' she asked in reply.

'No,' he replied. 'They separated, but my father loved my mother too much to let her go completely. It was his one dream that she would come back to him.'

'To Jahara?' Erith questioned, loving this moment of Dom telling her more than he ever had before.

'It was where they lived at the start of their marriage,' he revealed. 'But my sister was no more than six months old when my mother declared the she could live nowhere but in France, and left, taking Marguerite with her.'

Erith was silent for a moment or two as she digested what Dom had told her. And her interest mostly in him, 'But your father followed her to France?' she queried, realising that he must have done for Dom to have subsequently come into the world.

But, 'No,' he contradicted her. 'He loved her, but he would never leave Jahara. It was six years before he saw either her or Marguerite again.'

'Your mother—she still loved him?'

'She must have done. She returned to Peru to try again—and in due time I arrived. The next time she decided that she must live in France, though, my father insisted that she must leave me behind.'

'Oh, good heavens!' Erith exclaimed softly, adding, 'He must have thought the world of her.'

'He grew more and more embittered when, having been certain she would never go if it meant leaving her son behind, he found she did exactly that.'

Erith's feelings went out to his father. She wanted to say, oh, the poor man, but she stayed quiet, and a few silent seconds passed during which she felt a strange sort of empathy with the man opposite envelop her. A few more seconds of shared empathy passed, then, 'Did your mother never return again?' she asked quietly.

'Not even for his funeral when years later, embittered, as I mentioned, he died in an accident with some farm machinery—an accident that should never have happened.'

Erith was silent, this time as she wondered if Dom was saying that it was his belief that his father had grown so tired of waiting for the wife he loved to return that he had been careless about the machinery—on purpose.

Then she forgot that there might be any question mark over the way his father had died, for Dom seemed to be suddenly looking at her intently, when, not waiting for her to say anything, all at once he asked, 'What is your view, Erith? Do you think a woman should stay in her husband's country for love?'

'I . . .' she began, and halted. She looked down at her now empty plate, and knew for herself, should the man she loved ask her, she would stay with him in any land he chose. Even if that land did not house an idyllic spot such as Jahara, then if her love was returned, she would never want to leave.

'Well?' he queried when she had hesitated too long.

Erith flicked her glance back to him, and saw that his grey eyes seemed watchful somehow. For a few panicky moments she wondered if he had guessed how she felt about him, but then realised that he could have no idea, for, if he had, then she could be sure he would have kept off the topic of love entirely.

'I would have thought,' she began slowly, as she tried to give a straight, impartial reply, 'that it might not come to that if—from the start—there was total honesty between the two people involved.'

'Honesty?' questioned Dom, his tone suddenly sharp and causing her to realise she had offended him by, without meaning to, intimating that his parents were dishonest.

'I didn't mean your parents, particularly,' she hastened to assure him, starting to feel uncomfortable but at pains still to be as straight as she could. 'Although,' she qualified as she realised that his mother had probably had doubts about living elsewhere than France when she had married her Peruvian, 'it seems to me that a lot of unhappiness might have been prevented had they openly discussed beforehand any problems that could arise.'

'Honesty obviously means a lot to you?' Dom suggested, a shade stiffly, Erith thought.

'It's the basis for any sound relationship, isn't it?' she commented, but she knew when he didn't answer that any empathy she had imagined there being between them was gone.

For the next thirty seconds Erith blamed herself for that state of affairs. OK, so he had asked her opinion on whether a woman should stay in her husband's country for love, but had she needed to bore him with her pious platitudes on honesty?

'When did your sister return to Peru?' she tried for a slight change of subject—she just didn't want to be bad friends with Dom. Soon she would be back in England.

At first, though, she thought she had so bored him that he was not going to answer. He certainly seemed a man deep in thought, anyhow. But, when Erith was just beginning to hate herself if any comment she had made had sent him to dwell sadly on his parents, he suddenly roused himself to be aware that there was a question going unanswered.

'Marguerite came to Jahara often as a child,' he replied, breaking away from his own thoughts to tell her. 'She was seventeen and at Jahara when she fell in love with a visiting diplomat.'

'Was he the man she married?'

'*Si,*' Dom confirmed evenly. 'She married him, had Filipo, and later fell out of love with her husband.' Erith had known that Filipo's parents were divorced. But, when she might have asked a question or two about Marguerite, he asked abruptly, 'Would you like coffee?'

Erith knew then that he was as bored with this change of subject as he had been with her little homily about honesty. The time had come, it seemed, for her to go to bed.

'No, thanks,' she smiled, and kept on smiling as she added, 'That was a delicious meal. But now, would you mind if I turned in?'

His answer was to get courteously to his feet. Less than a second later, Erith rose too. 'Goodnight,' he bade her coolly.

'Goodnight,' she replied quietly, and felt quite bereft when, for once without an escort, she made her solitary way out of the dining-room.

It could have been, of course, that he had remained at the table because he was gasping for a cup of coffee, she fretted, as she made her way up to her room. But it wasn't that, she knew it wasn't.

Why he had stayed behind was a mystery to her, but love, she realised, had made her acutely sensitive where he was concerned. And she just knew that suddenly, Domengo de Zarmoza most definitely was a man with a great deal on his mind.

CHAPTER EIGHT

AFTER a tormented night spent in only fitful sleep, Erith was awake again at dawn with her thoughts once more on the man who held her heart. It was little short of a miracle, in her view, that Dom seemed to have no idea of the depth of her feelings for him.

More than a miracle, she decided, when she considered how eagerly she had clung when she had been in his arms. Warm colour surged to her face, but it quickly faded when harsh spiteful spikes of jealousy bombarded her as she began to realise that maybe there was a good reason why Dom had seen nothing out of the ordinary in the way she had clung to him. Maybe, those wounding thoughts crucified her, he had not discerned how very much he meant to her because he was only ever used to any female he held in his arms giving him total and wholehearted response.

When suddenly the pain from such contemplations became untenable, Erith, trying desperately hard to push such thoughts from her, shot out of bed and busied herself getting showered and dressed. She had just run a comb through her hair when someone knocked on her door.

Barefooted and imagining that perhaps room service had probably brought someone's breakfast to the wrong room, she went swiftly to answer it. As she pulled the door open with one hand, she pushed her long hair back from her face with the other.

That action, though, seemed to freeze midway when she discovered that it was not a member of the hotel

staff who stood there, but Dom. 'Oh—er—hello,' she
greeted him, her voice husky in her surprise. 'I—er...'
she tried to follow through, but discovered that to have
Dom scrutinising her clear, make-up-free complexion,
not to mention the fact that she was more than a little
shaken to see him there so unexpectedly, seemed to have
sent her thought processes into hibernation.

Not so him, however, though she had never known
him stuck for words in any language. 'Good morning,'
he greeted her coolly, transferring his gaze to her shining
Titian locks. 'Might I suggest you take an early breakfast
this morning?'

Abruptly Erith's brain became active. From what she
knew of him, she felt certain he would not, already
shaved, bathed and clothed in a lightweight suit at this
hour, come to her room to make such a request without
some good reason.

His cool tone, though, tipped her off that he was
feeling no more friendly this morning than he had been
when they had parted last night. Pride arrived in massive
quantities. 'Any particular reason why I should?' she
asked—a touch arrogantly, she had to admit.

He took but a couple of seconds to knock the legs of
arrogance from under her. 'We're flying to Lima today,'
he announced. 'I should like to be en route for the airport
by eight-thirty.'

If she had just been served a body blow, Erith felt she
could not have felt more wounded. Quite plainly, Dom
had seen that she cared for him. This, by escorting her
to Lima, and presumably thereafter putting her on a
plane bound for England, was his clean-cut way of
dealing with her unwanted love.

Never was Erith more glad of that pride that remained long enough for her to be able to appear, outwardly, totally unconcerned by what she had understood.
'I can be ready be seven-thirty, if need be,' she heard

the proud person who fronted the hurt in her say with a shrug, and even dared, 'But why the rush?'

His answer was not only to make her overwhelmingly glad that she had kept her cool and had not, as she felt like doing, crumpled. For it seemed that she was wrong in her thoughts about what lay behind his decision that they fly to Lima, and her green eyes were shooting wide in fresh surprise when he told her 'I know the exact location of your stepsister and Filipo.'

'You ...' Her voice petered out, so startled was she to hear that, when she had not expected to. 'I see,' she murmured slowly as she played for time while she got her thoughts together. 'You—er—mean... that you know definitely that they won't now be coming to Lake Titicaca?' She felt that the sentence she managed to bring out was fairly clear.

'Exactly,' he replied levelly.

It was as much then as she needed to know. 'I'll go down to breakfast straight away,' she told him.

She felt she loved him and hated him both at the same time when he drawled, 'It might be an idea to put something on your feet first,' and left her. As far as Erith was aware, he hadn't so much as given her bare toes a glance!

As he had wanted, they were on the road by eight-thirty. And, with Dom seeming to be heavily engaged with his own thoughts, Erith felt she would cut out her tongue before she would try and make conversation with him.

In actual fact, though, she could not have said her thoughts were all that light either. She had been shaken to realise that word must have reached him as to the definite whereabouts of Audra and Filipo, but she had been even more shaken when it had soon afterwards dawned on her that she would no sooner have met up with Audra than she would be flying home.

Consequently, there was an ache in Erith that was almost like a physical pain when she and Dom caught the plane for Lima at Juliaca. Any relief she might have felt a few hours earlier that the secret of her love for him was still safe had long since evaporated. Without doubt, she was still extremely glad that their purpose in flying to Lima was not on account of him knowing of her love and finding it tiresome, but because of his latest intelligence about Audra and Filipo. But Erith just didn't know how she was going to be able to face parting from him permanently.

That thought of being permanently apart from him, of never, ever seeing him again, was all at once too dreadful to contemplate. And suddenly she found she was breaking into speech—anything to keep such terrible, desolate thoughts at bay.

'Do—er—Audra and Filipo—er—by any chance know that we're on our way to Lima?' she asked suddenly.

Dom turned his aristocratic head a fraction, and Erith thought his grey-eyed look cool, as he replied curtly, 'They aren't in Lima.'

'They aren't!' she exclaimed in astonishment, wondering what on earth they were chasing to Lima for if the couple they were going to see weren't there. 'But you said——'

'I never said they were in Lima,' he cut her off shortly, as if daring her to call him a liar.

'No, but...' She broke off, that curt and totally-fed-up-with-her note in his voice whipping her up to find another helping of pride. It was that pride alone, nudging her to feel that no man, no matter how much loved, was going to show himself fed up with her and expect her to fall on his neck—not that Dom looked as if he expected anything of the kind—that was responsible for *her* tone. If his voice had been cool, then her voice was a decided few degrees cooler when she asked, 'Perhaps, *señor*, you could tell me where it is, exactly, that they are?'

Grief, she thought, as his gaze, all at once arctic at her cold tone, swept over her. 'In Trujillo,' he clipped.

'And where might Trujillo be?' she took the bit between her teeth to question.

She remained stubbornly determined when, flicking her a superior look down his straight nose, he supplied icily, 'North of Lima,' and turned from her to stare straight ahead.

It did nothing for her sudden attack of stubbornness to receive his unspoken message that it would please him very much if she would just shut up, for another question was soon on the tip of her tongue. She owned that, while having been confused for quite a lot of the time since discovering that she loved him, she was now confused about what in creation was happening, or was going to happen.

'Are we going on to Trujillo, then?' she put what she thought was a perfectly understandable question—and received a most definite long-suffering look for her trouble.

'Trujillo,' he stated, as if trying hard to keep his voice even, 'is only a forty-five-minute flight from Lima.'

'Yes, but——'

'When we get to Lima,' he spoke over the top of her voice as if he had never heard her, 'I shall ring Filipo, and he will come to us.'

Love Domengo de Zarmoza though she might, that didn't mean she couldn't hate the arrogant swine he could be at times too, Erith thought crossly. Surely it was only natural that she should ask a few questions, for goodness sake! What did he think she was, some—some zombie!

For a few minutes more Erith silently fumed about the bossy brute sitting next to her. It was her view, as she remembered that Filipo no longer worked for his uncle, that Dom was being particularly bossy. It just wouldn't occur to him, would it, to so much as *consider* that any command to Filipo of 'come at once to Lima' might not be obeyed!

That thought provoked another, and again Erith was breaking the silence with a question. 'You—didn't think that, maybe, it might have been an idea to ring Filipo from Lake Titicaca?' she asked, and at the hostile look Dom gave her she wondered how she had dared. Quite plainly, he didn't care to have anything he did or did not do questioned.

To her surprise, though, as she was starting to think that he was going to let her run for her answer, he suddenly stated—if not very willingly, 'It—will be—easier, from Lima.'

From that Erith guessed that, just as there were no international lines from Lake Titicaca, perhaps national lines for trunk calls were a bit sparse too. 'I see,' she murmured, and felt the first stirrings of worry over her stepsister. 'But,' she began after a moment, 'will Audra come to Lima with Filipo?'

'Of course!' he replied tersely, just as if he had no doubt about that whatsoever. And before she could challenge how could he be so sure, 'Fasten your seatbelt,' he instructed, 'we're landing.'

Thoughts of Audra faded from Erith's mind as memory of the flight she had previously taken with him played back in her mind. He had fastened her seatbelt for her then, and she remembered she had felt protected by him.

Dom informed her, as he hailed a taxi, that they would book into a hotel and be comfortable while they waited for Filipo and her stepsister to arrive. Erith didn't want to book into a hotel, but she didn't know either what it was she did want, other than just that she would have settled for just feeling good inside again—as she had on that flight from Arequipa to Juliaca.

But, since she supposed that to check into a hotel and relieve themselves of their luggage seemed the sensible thing to do, she sat silently in the taxi, feeling bruised by Dom's terse attitude with her, and tried to concentrate on other things.

From what she knew of Audra, she had the feeling that her stepsister was likely to object to being 'ordered' to Lima at her fiancé's uncle's bidding. Though, as Erith thought of how Jean had been almost demented while waiting to hear from her thoughtless daughter, the fact that Audra might object didn't bother her.

She was still trying to hide the hurt she felt at the hostile way Dom was treating her when the taxi dropped them off at a hotel in the Miraflores area of Lima. She thought of how they had laughed and loved together, and thought that perhaps it was as well that she would soon be leaving Peru. Despite Dom's brutish attitude, she still had some happy memories of her time with him. She wanted to keep those memories, not to have them tarnished by memories of how cold he could be when the mood was on him.

What conversation passed between Dom and the registration clerk, Erith could only guess at. But Dom turned to her as the clerk handed over a couple of keys, and easily switched to English, to comment. 'We'll go and check our rooms—they can bring our cases up later.'

Without a word, Erith fell into step beside him as they walked over to the lifts. Silently she stood with him while the lift they had stepped into zoomed upwards. She had nothing to say to him either as he escorted her out of the lift and to one of the doors in the corridor.

What she expected then, as she stood, her expression impassive, was that Dom would insert one of the keys into the lock, open the door for her—and leave her to

it. He did not do that, however, but, to set her heart
drumming, he looked long and steadily down into her
solemn green eyes. Then, to make her heart beat even
faster, 'Erith,' he said her name, and there was a husky
quality in his tone, a warmth there, she would swear it,
as he began, 'There's something I need—want—to say
to you...' only just then a maid ambled into sight
wheeling a trolley-load of fresh bedlinen and stopped at
a door only a few yards away. The next Erith knew, Dom
was looking momentarily distracted. And in the next
second, all sign of warmth went from him—if indeed
she hadn't imagined it in the first place—and, 'You look
tired,' he was telling her in that cold voice she was beginning to hate, and before she could tartly thank him
for the compliment, 'Go and rest!' he ordered in clipped
tones, and, pausing only to push a room key at her, he
abruptly turned round and headed back to the lifts.

Erith was still staring after him in a stunned fashion
when, clearly a man in need of some physical action, he
ignored the lift, to go striding to the stone stairway. Then,
while she still stood watching, without so much as a
backward glance he started down the stairs, two at a
time.

Her eyes were still glued to the stairs, Dom long since
gone from her sight, when she became aware that the
lift was coming to a halt at the floor she was on. What
happened then, as she drew her eyes away from the
stairhead to glance over to the lifts, was little short of
astonishing.

If she had been stunned by Dom's recent behaviour,
though, then stunned didn't begin to cover how she felt
when the lift doors opened and a tall and slender blonde
stepped out.

'Audra!' Erith gasped, as she took several disbelieving paces towards the blonde.

'Erith!' the blonde exclaimed, her tone even more disbelieving. 'What on earth are you doing here?'

'I can't believe... What...? Did Dom phone you after all to...?'

'Dom?' Audra, the first to recover, took up while Erith was still getting over her shock at seeing her stepsister so unexpectedly. 'Are you talking of Domengo de Zarmoza?'

Speechlessly Erith nodded. Then, finding her voice again, 'He's been helping me try to find you. We've been everywhere looking for you,' she informed Audra, the 'everywhere' exaggeration permissible, she felt, in the shock of seeing her so unexpectedly.

But a fresh shock awaited her. What she expected her stepsister to say in answer to that, she wasn't quite sure, most likely some anxious question as to why she had been looking for her, and was her mother all right? But Audra almost floored her when, leaving such questions for the moment, she questioned instead, 'You say Domengo de Zarmoza has been helping you look for me?' and as Erith again nodded, 'Now, isn't that strange?' she drawled, and dropped a mammoth bombshell as she added, 'Especially when you consider that he's known exactly where I was since the day four months ago when he almost threw me and his nephew out of Jahara.'

'What...?' Erith gasped faintly, her jaw dropping. 'But—but...' It was no good, she was so shaken by what Audra had just said that she just couldn't begin to think straight.

She was, therefore, rather grateful when her stepsister took charge. 'We can't talk here,' she decreed. 'We'll go to my room.'

A few minutes later, Erith was seated in a chair in her stepsister's room, and was thankful to find that her head was starting to clear. Somebody, she realised, had to be lying, and that someone just had to be Audra. Why Audra should be lying wasn't apparent to Erith, but, despite the grim way Dom had been with her that day, she did, as she had told him, trust him utterly and completely.

Though before she could begin to question her step-sister, Audra first had a few questions of her own, starting with, 'What are you doing so far away from home, anyway?'

'Your mother—and my father—were worried about you,' Erith replied.

'Worried? Heavens, I've been able to take care of myself since I was about seventeen!' Audra scorned, and as light suddenly dawned, 'Hell's bells, they didn't send you to come looking for me?' she exclaimed.

It did not escape Erith's notice that her stepsister, only a few months older than herself, seemed to consider her still wet behind the ears. But she chose to ignore the intended jibe, as she reminded her, 'You went off with some man named Nick, and the next your mother knows, from the only letter she's received, is that you're en-gaged to some man called Filipo.'

'Life's been a bit—hectic,' Audra shrugged, about the nearest she was going to come to feeling in any way regretful for the worry she had caused. Erith realised, as Audra went on to ask, 'When did you arrive in Peru?'

'A couple of weeks ago,' she replied, two short weeks seeming incredible. Though having been so much in Dom's company, she felt that she had known him forever.

'You traced me through Dom de Zarmoza?' Audra queried.

'It's a long story,' Erith replied, having not *traced* her at all, but more 'bumped into her'. 'The thing is, you said that he'd known where you were ever since the day you left Jahara?' Erith was feeling more composed then than she had as she waited, fully expecting that Audra, having made her dramatic statement, would now start to prevaricate.

But, with not a glimmer of prevarication, 'So he has,' she confirmed.

'But how can he have known where you were?' Erith pressed. While she held no particular brief for Audra, it seemed important somehow that she defend Dom from Audra's slur that he was a liar. 'You've been moving around the country,' she pointed out, 'and it doesn't——'

'Who says I've been moving around the country?' Audra wanted to know.

'Dom said. You and Filipo have been touring. You've——'

'It seems to me that Dom has been telling you a whole lot of little porkies,' Audra butted in, and while Erith was getting ready to protest vehemently that she was sure that Dom had never told her so much as a single solitary lie, Audra was asking, 'Now why, I wonder, would he do that?'

'I... He hasn't... He's no need to lie. He...' Erith broke off at the speculative light that suddenly came into her stepsister's eyes. But Erith was shaken to forget her defence of him when abruptly Audra asked,

'Have you been to bed with him?'

'No!' she denied sharply, but could do nothing about the warm colour that flooded her face at how touch-and-go that state of affairs had been.

'But he's tried it on, hasn't he?' Audra did not flinch from asking.

'What's that got to do with anything?' Erith questioned, starting to feel a little peeved with her stepsister.

'A hell of a lot, I'd say,' Audra replied, and, to strike a chill at Erith's heart, 'Some men will stop at nothing to get a woman into bed with them.'

Not Dom, Erith wanted to tell her, but suddenly she felt her world begin to crumble. She *had* trusted him, utterly and completely, but all at once she no longer felt she was on sturdy ground.

'Anyhow,' she passed over that which she did not wish to discuss with her stepsister, and challenged shortly instead, 'What proof have you that Dom has known where you were the whole of these last two weeks?'

'I,' Audra shrugged, 'don't need it. But, if *you* want proof, I'll give you Filipo's *mamá's* telephone number.'

'Marguerite...?'

'The same,' Audra agreed, and went on, 'To fill you in, a couple of months after Filipo ceased working in Chimbote we moved to a rented property in Trujillo. His mother was most cut up about him not working for her brother any more and was always on the phone to Filipo about it. Which, I'd say, makes it more than likely that she was always on the phone to her brother about it too— no doubt at the same time bewailing the fact that her son had set up house with me. Anyhow, it was Marguerite's turn to receive a telephone call when your double-dealing "friend" wanted Filipo's new address and telephone number.'

'He was trying to find you!' Erith exclaimed at once.

'He knew, from Marguerite, every movement we made!' Audra denied any suggestion that there had been any difficulty in knowing their whereabouts. 'Dammit, that woman was never off the phone—I should know, I spoke to her—be it briefly—most days!'

Silence filled the room as Erith took in what Audra had said. Then, as an awful feeling of having been totally duped started to claw for a hold, hope waged a battle that perhaps Audra was inventing *some* of it, and that it could be that it was only this morning, or at the earliest last night, that Dom had discovered where Filipo and Audra were living.

'When was this?' she quickly asked one of the many questions that rushed to the fore. 'When was it, have you any idea, when D-Dom phoned Marguerite to ask for your address?'

'I've more than an idea! I can tell you exactly,' Audra answered. 'It was two weeks ago tomorrow.' She went on to relate how it seemed that Marguerite had not taken to her living with her son very well, which was why Audra had persuaded Filipo—who was not averse either to quite frequently telephoning his mother—to have a week away from their apartment. They had returned on that Tuesday to hear the phone ringing—Marguerite on the line—as they had let themselves back into the flat.

All hope that she had not been totally hoodwinked abruptly left Erith. That particular Tuesday in question was the day after her arrival in Peru—the very day, in fact, that she had met Dom. He had known from the very beginning, as Audra had said, exactly where Audra was. The whole time he had been telling her that her stepsister was touring the country, he had been deceiving her, lying to her, in fact.

Knowing that, however, a ray of hope in Erith refused to be doused. 'You're sure that Marguerite definitely gave Dom your address?' she just had to have another last stab at finding some way to exonerate the man she loved.

'She's so anxious for her brother to take Filipo back into the firm that there's no way she'd hold back on anything he wanted to know,' Audra promptly hit the last rays of hope soundly on the head.

Hurt started to sear Erith that Dom could have lied to her so. She knew that Audra was looking at her, and needing to hide her hurt from the world she got up from her chair and went to stare unseeing out of the window.

'Marguerite obviously thought Dom wanted your address and phone number—so he could contact Filipo to discuss his rejoining the firm,' she documented as she finally let go all hope that Domengo de Zarmoza had not been having a very amusing time at her expense.

'If he did he neither rang nor wrote to Filipo,' Audra supplied—and offered, 'From what you've said, it seems to me that he only wanted to know where we were so he could keep tabs on our movements. It wouldn't do at all, would it, if, coincidence being what it is, we met up before he was ready?'

Erith was by then having the hardest work not to break down, that Dom could treat her so cavalierly. She was hurting more than she had ever hurt in her life. But, as she grabbed at a stray wisp of strength, she determined that only she was going to know it. Which left her, if she was not going to make a fool of herself in front of Audra, to think about anything other than the man who must have been laughing up his sleeve—both sleeves— this past fortnight.

But, with the tall Peruvian dominating so much of her mind, Erith did not get further in her thoughts than his nephew. He would do, she thought, and promptly asked Audra, 'Is Filipo with you in Lima?'

'Like hell he is!' Audra surprised her by replying in no uncertain terms. 'I got out and left him to it when yesterday, being a little short of funds, I asked him for some money, and he had the nerve to tell me he's insolvent!'

'Insolvent?' Erith queried, glad to have something other than Dom to pin her thoughts on.

'Temporarily, I should have said,' Audra corrected. 'I'm on my beam ends too, so I need a temporarily insolvent lover like I need a hole in the head. I'd got enough for a plane ticket this far,' she added, and Erith came near to liking her when, her spirit clearly un-daunted, she suddenly smiled and said, 'I knew my good fortune wouldn't desert me. Here *you* are!'

From that, Erith realised that Audra—if she was as penniless as she had stated—was of the opinion that she could pay her hotel bill for her. 'It's all over between you and Filipo, then?' she guessed. 'You've broken your engagement?'

'Good lord, we were never engaged!' Audra exclaimed. 'Filipo asked me outright to be his mistress. He only ever wanted to bed me—and while he'd got ample funds that suited me fine,' she said with staggering frankness. 'But . . .'

'But when he went broke, you decided you didn't like him so much after all?'

'Something like that,' Audra replied carelessly, and silence fell between them as Audra became occupied with her own thoughts and Erith tried to avoid hers—which began with how Audra had lied to her mother by writing that she was engaged to Filipo.

From there, in natural and painful progression, Erith could not stop thinking of Dom—and the many lies he had told. She remembered once seeking him out in his study to enquire if he'd received any answers to his enquiries as to Audra's whereabouts. 'You must have patience, *señorita*,' he had told her. Had he taken her for a ride! She should never have listened to him, she realised, when roaring in came the memory of that evening after dinner at Jahara when she had been packing with the intention of returning to England. 'I've just taken a phone call,' he had lyingly come to her room to tell her. 'Apparently Filipo has been seen in Arequipa.'

'Have you and Filipo been in Arequipa recently?' she asked Audra as the question sprang to her lips.

'Arequipa's way down in the south. Neither Filipo nor I have been further south than Jahara since we met,' Audra replied, and another knife twisted in Erith.

Oh, had *she* been a gullible idiot! She had believed every dreadful lie Dom had told her. Pain racked her as she thought of how, not an hour ago, he'd made her heart beat the faster when 'Erith,' he'd said, warmly, she'd thought, 'there's something I need—want—to say to you...' My stars, she'd bet there was something, some lying something he wanted to say to her.

She swallowed hard on a knot of emotion, and was weakened as she remembered his lovemaking, his kisses, the way he had desired her. Had he meant to lie again? Was it as Audra said, that some men would stop at nothing to get a woman into bed with them? Erith remembered too how Audra had told her Filipo had asked her outright to be his mistress. Was that what Dom was about with his 'There's something I need—want—to say to you...'? Had he been about to ask her to be *his* mistress? Erith thought of the wild way she had responded to him, and knew that she was weak where he was concerned. But was that what she wanted—a relationship like the one which Audra had had with Filipo?

Everything in her screamed out against something that seemed suddenly sordid. She loved Dom, but did she want only to be his mistress—for a brief while? From what she could make out, there had been no place for love in what had been between Audra and her lover— did she want the same sort of 'clinical' relationship?

The answer to that question was all at once painfully clear—and Erith knew at that exact moment what she was going to do. She loved Dom; despite what he had done, she seemed unable to stop loving him. But, with everything starting to point to the fact that it seemed he had been leading up to ask her to be his mistress, she knew that that role was not for her.

'I'm going back to England!' she suddenly announced to Audra. Her heart might still be his, but how, if Audra's experience with Filipo was anything to go by, could she live with him for even that brief while, when anything they did have going for them was built on a foundation of lies?

'What—now? Today?' Audra exclaimed, startled.

'If I can get a flight,' Erith told her calmly.

She realised she'd have company when, after less than two seconds' thought, Audra declared, 'I might as well come with you.'

Audra was in a talkative mood on the way to the airport—Erith was not. It hadn't taken them long to leave the hotel, she reflected as the taxi headed in the direction of the airport. Audra had been only half unpacked anyway, so it had only taken minutes to, as she put it, 'throw the rest of my things into my case'.

Erith was feeling so bewildered and unhappy by all that had happened by that time she would not have cared had she had to leave Peru without her belongings. It didn't come to that, however, because Audra reminded her that she had her room key, and was of the opinion—when acquainted with the fact that Erith, newly arrived, had last seen her luggage downstairs—that a porter would have brought her case to her room by then.

She was proved right, though, as Erith observed that the accommodation which Dom had booked her into was a suite, rather than a room, so the feeling of being about to break down overtook her again. Dom, by the look of it, wanted her to be as comfortable out of bed as in it. Quickly she grabbed up her case, and there seemed nothing more to do then than pray with all she had that she did not bump into him as she left.

She had not bumped into him, and she got out of the taxi at the airport swamped by regret that she had not seen him, while at the same time she acknowledged that she was feeling too sick at heart to know what she wanted any more.

Erith left it to Audra to make enquiries about a flight to England, and sitting by herself with their luggage she tried, unsuccessfully, to fathom why Dom had brought her to Lima. He had been speaking the truth about Filipo's being in Trujillo, she realised, and suddenly found she was again weakening against him.

Hell's bells—she tried to get angry—was she so pathetic that she wanted to stay around to hear yet more of his lies? It was for certain, whatever his purpose in bringing her to Lima was, that he had no intention of ringing Filipo from there ordering him to take the next plane.

By the time Audra came back to where she was sitting, Erith had firmly ejected from her mind every memory of the times Dom had made her smile, or been gentle with her, or protective of her. Every action, every move, had been made to make her fall for him, and she—she had, and he was a rat. She remembered then how he'd said that he'd never made love to a virgin, and guessed she had no need to think further.

'Is there a flight soon?' She jerked her thoughts away from him to look up at Audra.

'There is, any time now—but there's a bit of a snag,' Audra replied, and, taking the seat next to her, she went into more detail.

Twenty minutes later, the snag Audra had spoken of being that it seemed that between them they had air-fare enough only for one, they stood at the entrance of the departure lounge.

It was totally unexpected to Erith that Audra should lean forward and give her a quick hug and a kiss on the cheek. Then they both took a step back.

'See you!' said Audra.

'Bye,' said Erith.

Simultaneously they turned around, Audra to quickly disappear as she passed out of sight to go through the requisite pre-boarding procedures, Erith to turn—and feel her whole being come alive. For she found herself staring straight up into the strangely haunted-looking face of none other than Domengo de Zarmoza.

'Erith!' he called her name, his voice sounding hoarse and like that of a wounded man. 'I thought you'd gone!' he breathed, and while her heart leapt wildly, she saw that he appeared to be desperately shaken that it might have been so—that she, and not Audra, had taken the flight.

Dom! Erith almost cried his name. But that was before the reality of the situation suddenly jetted in. And suddenly she was more furious than she had ever been in her life. The swine, the diabolical swine! she thought, outraged, as she added 'actor' to the list of his lying attributes. Even at this late stage he wasn't of a mind to give up on the two weeks' work he'd put in on softening her up.

'No, I didn't go,' she told him while she fought hard to contain the rage that had started to explode within her. But as she thought of his treachery, his deceit, suddenly she knew she had no hope of keeping her fury under control. Red mists of outrage were starting to swim before her eyes all at once, and as her rage boiled over, Erith had the answer, if she needed it, to what she would do if ever she saw him again.

Regardless that there were people still walking about, regardless that they could be seen by anyone who glanced in their direction, suddenly she went totally out of control. She was not conscious of anyone else being around, though, when thoughts of his duplicity fused with the unbearable hurt she was suffering, and like lightning her right hand suddenly rocketed through the air, and with all the force she was capable of Erith caught him a wickedly stinging blow on the side of his face.

CHAPTER NINE

ERITH saw Dom's head jerk back from the force of the blow she served him, but, although both his hands shot out to her, he did not reply in kind. Instead he took hold of her upper arms, though whether to keep her from hitting him again or just to keep her there, she did not know.

Then, as she drew a convulsive breath as she fought for self-control, Dom uttered shakenly, 'Thank God you're still here! When I learned you'd left the hotel with your stepsister, I thought that you'd both be gone!'

More self-control was arriving by the moment as Erith stared at him. She thought there seemed a tinge of grey to his colour, as though he was a man who was, or had been, under some stress. Then it started to register that he somehow knew she had met Audra. But she had no intention of asking him anything—she'd heard more than enough lies roll off his tongue.

'As you know,' she told him coldly, 'I had air-fare only for one. Audra didn't have that much.'

'So you gave her your fare, and stayed,' he documented, his voice, in contrast to hers, holding a warm note. 'Why?' he asked, his eyes watching her every expression. And when she did not answer, 'Was it because you wanted to—that you stayed'

'I stayed because Audra's mother will be better for seeing her,' Erith replied, and as the implication behind his words suddenly sank in, once again she wanted to hammer the daylights out of him. This time, though— and it had nothing to do with the fact that he still had a firm grip on her upper arms—she did not physically lash out at him, but instead she erupted to demand, 'What the hell's it got to do with you anyway?'

She was glaring at him when he surprised her by not firing up in return but replying mildly, 'Everything.' The heat of her anger started to die. It was rapidly resurrected when he added, 'I told you I had something I wanted to say to you. I——'

'A confession, no doubt!' Erith burst in hotly—it was beneath her dignity to mention that she knew what he wanted to say had nothing to do with a confession, but was a quest that he join her in her bed for a brief month or two.

But, 'A confession—of sorts,' he agreed. And, while she was still staring coldly at him, he urged, to her amazement, 'Come with me. Hear me out, and then if you still hate my guts I'll give you your air-fare back to England, and——'

'Give?' she exploded proudly, though some part of her became a little less tense that he seemed under no illusion that she did anything but hate him.

'Lend, if you prefer.' He made a small impatient movement. Then, as somebody jostled by, they both seemed to become aware that they were not alone, but stood blocking the way at a busy airport.

'Where are you suggesting we go for this "confession—of sorts"?' Erith questioned acidly, realising only then that she couldn't have been thinking at all clearly when she'd allowed Audra to persuade her that it would be better if she was the one to return to England. Erith had thought vaguely in terms of throwing herself on the mercy of the British Consul in Lima and of explaining how her money had been stolen in Cuzco. Which meant, anyway, that she'd have to leave the airport at some time.

'Anywhere you wish,' Dom replied, moving her out of the way of someone else who wanted to get past. 'Though it seems to me that it might be an idea if we were somewhere more—comfortable—than here.'

'Somewhere like a suite in a hotel in Miraflores, perhaps?' Erith questioned, instantly wary.

'I don't blame you for being suspicious,' Dom took her aback by telling her gently. 'And it's true that I should like to—be private—for what I have to say to you.'

'I'll bet you would!'

He ignored her comment, and went on, 'Of course, if you wish it, we will leave the door into the corridor open.'

'That sounds like a good idea,' Erith mumbled, chary still but discovering, since she was going to have to leave the airport anyway, that that seemed to be that. She caught a brief glimpse of what appeared to be relief on his face, then, while keeping a hold on her, he hunted up and collected her suitcase, and took her outside to claim a taxi.

Erith could not have said quite what her thoughts and feelings were during that taxi ride back to the hotel. She was, she owned, weak in the extreme to have agreed to go anywhere with him. What was there for her to hear anyway—she had guessed at it all, hadn't she?

Wretched, lying hound! His confession, of sorts, she knew full well would be all about not telling her—when he'd known all the time—where Audra was. From there, Erith didn't doubt, she would be on the receiving end of a proposition that she be his mistress.

If she was silent on that taxi ride, then so too was the man by her side. Silent—and, she felt, tense. Though what he had to be tense about she didn't know, as he escorted her into the hotel and, claiming her key, up in the lift.

The tension she felt in him, however, communicated itself to her once they were in the sitting-room of the suite, and Erith suddenly started to get cross not only with him, but herself too.

'If you'd care to be seated, Erith?' he suggested, as he placed her case at the rear of one of the two small settees in the room.

'I will in a minute!' she told him shortly, and first went to close the outer door which he had left open. She knew in advance how all this was going to end, but whatever else she didn't know about the man to whom she had so crazily given her heart, there was something that she inherently did know—that he would not resort to rape when she told him that, thanks all the same, but she had no intention of agreeing to be his temporary bedfellow.

Having closed the outer door, Erith went over to one of the settees and sat down. She smiled a phoney smile and, with equally phoney sweetness, murmured, 'It's "confession" time!'

Then she had the smile wiped straight off her face when, after giving her a long, level look, Dom lowered his tall length on to the settee opposite, and replied evenly, 'It's something, Erith, that you still trust me.'

'So what's this you want me to hear?' she questioned tartly, having not put into words herself that she still trusted him but realising that by her action in closing the door—keeping the outside world out—it must seem that she still did.

'I've—lied to you.'

'You can say that again!' she erupted, and, fully expecting to see his hostility arrive in full force, she was surprised that not a smattering of hostility came into his expression. But, as he eyed her levelly, it seemed that he was ready to take everything that she threw at him! Which Erith found more than a little shaking.

'At first, I didn't know why I had lied to you,' he began. She pulled herself together to hope he didn't think it was her place to tell him.

'Lust!' she suggested, by way of a hint.

'Lust had nothing to do with it!' he denied sharply.

'You *do* surprise me!' Erith tossed at him sarcastically,

'No more than I've been surprised by myself, and my own actions since meeting you,' he ignored her sarcasm to tell her. 'Since meeting you . . .' He broke off, his jaw working. Then, after a tense kind of pause, he changed tack to tell her, 'I'm trying to be as honest with you as——'

'Honest!' she interrupted him sharply, her green eyes flashing as she dwelt on the many lies he had told her. 'You *are* leaving yourself wide open!'

'I've no cover now,' he responded promptly, 'and I know it. I want, need . . .' He broke off and paused again and if she didn't know better, Erith would have thought that he was a shade nervous. But, since that couldn't be, she stared hostilely at him—and waited. Then, quietly, he requested, 'If you'll allow me, Erith, I'll go back to the beginning, when——'

'Don't leave anything out on my account!' she invited belligerently. If her heart was banging against her ribs from just being in the same room with him, then only she was going to know it.

'Very well,' he said gravely, his expression sombre, everything about him suddenly seeming to convey that this conversation with her was of the utmost importance to him.

Indeed, there was something so deadly serious about the whole of his countenance that it communicated itself to her, and Erith could find no comment, sarcastic or otherwise, to insert. Silently she waited while Dom formed what he wanted to say. When he did begin to speak again, however, he had not gone back to the time when she and he had first met, but to the first time he had met Audra.

'As you know, I at one time employed my nephew in a management position in my boat firm in Chimbote,' he refreshed her memory. 'What you may not know, unless your stepsister has told you, is that shortly after he met her his work started to suffer so badly that I took a plane up there to see what was going on.'

From that, Erith had a fair idea that but for their kin relationship Dom would have dismissed Filipo without taking the trouble to personally fly to Chimbote. 'I—didn't know that. Audra didn't say,' she murmured, her tone quiet and, whether she knew it or not, encouraging him to go on.

'What I found when I saw Filipo was that he was in the initial throes of an affair, and that your stepsister was demanding that he forgo his work in favour of escorting her around town.'

'You met Audra in Chimbote?'

'I did,' Dom replied, 'and you'll forgive me, if you have any great affection for her, but since there must be only honesty now with everything I say to you, I have to say that I at once saw that she was far more interested in Filipo's wallet than she was in Filipo himself!'

'It was that obvious?' Erith asked, feeling embarrassed on her stepsister's behalf.

'I'm afraid so,' Dom replied, and added reluctantly, 'As I'm afraid it is a fact that, when your stepsister realised that I had a fatter wallet by far than Filipo, she showed quite an inclination to—um—be more my "friend" than his. Please do not feel uncomfortable on my account,' Dom added swiftly, as Erith, realising that Audra must have made quite a play for him, looked away. 'I didn't mean to upset you. I just wanted...'

'It's all right,' she recovered to tell him, and, wanting the subject changed, 'What did you do—about Filipo, and his work, I mean?'

'I instructed him to pull himself together, and left Chimbote. From there I travelled on to Europe to attend some business meetings. I returned to Jahara a couple of weeks later to find that your stepsister and Filipo were paying me a visit.'

'They—weren't invited?' Erith questioned.

Dom shook his head. 'They had arrived the day before, and Señora Garcia, familiar with Filipo from his many visits before, saw no reason to turn them away.'

From what had been said so far, it would not have surprised Erith to hear that Audra had been the one to instigate that visit. But, if Dom thought so too, he spared telling her. Erith realised then that he could not have been too pleased to have returned from what was probably an exhausting business trip abroad, to find Audra in residence. She somehow had a good idea that Audra would have been given polite but short shrift had she tried a second visit.

'Was that the time that Filipo quit his job?' she asked a question that seemed to follow naturally.

'It was,' Dom replied, and handed her some more of his new-found honesty when he added, 'Though to be truthful, I don't think I gave him much choice.' Then, leaning forward, he scrutinised Erith's face, then went on, 'However, having had what you might express as "something of a dust-up" with my nephew, I then had to endure weeks of my sister being constantly on the phone filling me in with the latest happenings of her son and "that woman".'

'So you did know—all the time—exactly where Audra and Filipo were?' Erith questioned very, very quietly.

And Dom was urging, very, very quickly, 'Please do not again lose the very fierce temper which until today

I only suspected you had. I wish to tell you everything if you will let me, and where it starts, for you and me,' he stated, unknowingly neutralising her temper more effectively with those last four words than with anything else he could have said.

'So?' she said, just that one word.

It was all the invitation he waited for. 'You, my dear, happened to arrive at a time when I'd just about had enough of the disruptive influences of Englishwomen.'

'Was that why you were so short-tempered with me?' she asked, not really needing an answer. With him losing one of his management team through Filipo's work going to pot when Audra had come on the scene—not to mention Marguerite's ringing him constantly, most likely at the same time, to bend his ear about Audra—she could see for herself that it was no wonder he'd had enough of Englishwomen.

'Are you going to allow me to apologise for being the way I was with you?' he questioned.

'You thought I was the same—er—type as my stepsister?'

'You showed me at once that you were not,' Dom declared instantly. 'I'd barely met you when you were proudly telling me that you were not penniless and that you had sufficient funds to pay for your return to England.' He paused then, and looking steadily into her large green eyes, 'Can you wonder, Erith, that I should feel a strange, nebulous something start to attack me?' he asked.

Her heart had accelerated a few beats when only a minute earlier he had called her 'my dear'. At his steady look, at his words, those words that seemed loaded with implication somehow, Erith's heartbeat began to race.

But, 'Oh?' she murmured, for all the world as though she was not more than idly curious. 'What sort of nebulous something?'

'I do not know,' he replied, 'or didn't—then. At first, all I knew was that the police had contacted me from Cuzco and told me how an English *señorita*, claiming to be related to my nephew's fiancée, had been the victim of a bag-snatcher. Frankly,' he went on, 'I saw no reason whatever to come to see you. It so happened, though, that I had to go to Cuzco about a business matter—a business matter which I finished in half the time I'd allowed. For no reason I then found that I was driving in the direction of your hotel.'

'You hadn't intended to come?'

Again Dom shook his head. 'Fate,' he replied with the first trace of a smile she had seen on him in a long while, 'must have been beckoning, even then.'

'Oh?' she murmured questioningly again, as she strove to keep her tone non-committal.

'Oh indeed,' he took up. 'I arrived at that hotel in Cuzco annoyed with myself for being there at all, and determined to serve you only the shortest of politenesses. But that was before I was confronted by a fantastically complexioned, green-eyed, stunning redhead, who was all pride and who—I could see straight away—was totally different from her stepsister.'

'Er—thank you for the—compliments,' Erith told him as she fought gallantly to keep herself from being charmed by him. 'But why lie to me? You couldn't have...' She broke off, then, realising that this was no time for her to start pussyfooting around the issue, 'You couldn't have felt *then* that you wouldn't—mind—er—having me for a—a bed-friend, so...'

'So why lie?' Dom asked gently, not denying that he wanted her for a bed-friend. 'I hardly knew myself. You'd said that you'd enough to pay your fare back to England, and I had the strangest feeling that I didn't want you to go. I decided later that my reluctance to see you go must stem from nothing more than curiosity to know why you had made the trip to my country in the first place.'

'But I told you why!' she reminded him.

'So you did,' he replied. 'So I found I was getting angry that after only one night in my country you wanted to leave.'

'That doesn't sound very logical,' Erith told him primly.

'I have grown of the opinion over these last two weeks,' he informed her, his eyes holding hers, 'that logic ceased to exist the moment I met you.'

'You've—always—sounded logical—to me,' Erith told him falteringly, the fact that he was refusing to let her look away having a great deal to do with her faltering words, she thought.

'Was it logical, when I wasn't even going to come to your hotel to see you, that, barely had I met you, I should to my amazement find that I'm inviting you into my home—or that I should discover I'm withholding information about where you would find your stepsister?'

'Why did you—initially?' she asked, certain in her own mind that she knew full well why he had withheld that information later when 'lust' had reared its ugly head.

'Initially,' he replied, 'I found that I wanted to know more of what goes on in your mind, more of your personality. Initially, I thought to delay telling you all you needed to know by only a few hours—and then I discovered that I was . . .' he paused for a moment before continuing, ' . . . that I was starting to like you, and that I just didn't want to do anything that would see you leaving on the next plane.'

Erith felt a frantic need to swallow hard on just hearing that Dom had begun to like her. But, if she was to walk out of here with a dignified 'No, thanks' after he'd come to the end of what he was saying, then she knew she had better start taking charge of the situation right here and now.

So she did not swallow, but, tilting her chin a fraction aggressively, she accused, 'You lied to me! I asked you outright if you had any news of Audra...'

'And I,' he took up, defeating the heat in her by his gentle look, 'to my own astonishment, told not one lie, but began on a whole trail of untruths.'

'B-because...' She broke off, wishing her brain were sharper. The trouble was, though, that with her heart playing silly fools inside her, and with Dom looking so kindly at her, her brain power seemed to be affected. 'You didn't—er—des...want me, then,' she managed to bring out eventually. 'So why...?'

'Why lie at that stage?' he finished for her. 'Believe me, I couldn't understand why myself. Lying, I promise you, normally has no part of me,' he told her sincerely, 'so the evasions and even downright untruths that started from almost the first moment of seeing you were the more astonishing to me. I have to confess, however, that at that very first dinner at Jahara I became very much— attracted—by the natural charm of you.'

Erith's eyes widened a fraction, and while she owned that she had not been aware that she had any natural charm, she could not deny the way her heart raced a few beats to hear that—that early on, Dom had been *attracted*!

It caused her to forget for a minute or two what this whole discussion was basically about, then, 'You—er— did?' she questioned.

'I am determined to tell you only the truth,' was her answer. Then he went on, 'Attracted by your personality as I was, though, it was at that same meal that I became quite furious when you had the nerve to tell me calmly that you wanted to return to England as soon as possible.'

'I remember!' she exclaimed. 'You were quite—nasty—when you asked if I had some man in England waiting for me.'

'How else should I be?' he questioned solemnly, and very nearly poleaxed her when, quietly, he added, 'I had never experienced the emotion—jealousy—before. I discovered then what a totally unreasoning emotion it is.'

'You were—*jealous*, that I—er—might have some man waiting for me in England?' Erith questioned, her eyes huge in her face.

'Oh, yes,' he murmured softly. 'I didn't acknowledge it for the emotion it was then, of course. At the time I was in a state of quite some bewilderment at my actions, I believe. Yet, even so, even knowing that I was behaving quite contrary to the way in which I more normally behaved, I seemed unable to put a stop to it. Without knowing why, I discovered that I wanted you to enjoy being in my home—in my country. Without knowing why, it annoyed me most extraordinarily when you said you wanted to leave. And, when I had in actual fact already phoned Marguerite and learned the exact location of Filipo—and his woman friend—I found, without knowing why, that I was keeping the information to myself.'

Erith's eyes were still large in her face as she heard him out to the end. She almost asked him if he knew now why. But suddenly some of her former brain power returned, and all at once she was angry, both with him and herself. For goodness' sake—she knew *why*! And as more pain started to bite that he was *still* deceiving her, she was suddenly erupting. 'You must take me for a complete idiot, *señor*!' She was on her feet—so too, *rapidly*, was he. 'You know full well *why*!' she stormed. 'It's been your aim to get me into bed ever since——'

His hands coming swiftly to capture her shoulders caused her to break off and take a hurried step backwards. The calves of her legs were up against the settee, and she could go no further when, his hands still on her shoulders, he softly gentled her, 'Quiet now.' Then, as she just looked at him and it seemed her short burst of temper was spent, 'Yes, I know *now* why—but I didn't know then,' he murmured. 'And yes, my dear, I desire you and want you, as you so genteelly put it, to be my bed-friend.' Erith gave an abrupt movement and tried to pull out of his hold, but his hold was fast, and he was looking tenderly down into her unhappy green eyes. 'But, my darling,' he told her, 'there's more to it than that—much, much more.'

His 'my darling' defeated her, and she felt completely lost when, with her whole being tingling from his touch, she could only say a bewildered, 'I—don't understand.'

Dom's answer was to put an arm around her and to manoeuvre her until she was sitting back down on the settee. Then he sat down beside her and, taking hold of both her hands, he said quietly, 'I don't expect you do. I didn't understand or accept what had happened to me myself until very recently.'

The feel of his hands on hers was of no help in the strenuous efforts which Erith was making to get herself together. Nor was his closeness on the small settee any help either. And, if anything, she was feeling more bewildered than ever as, striving with all she had for a cool note, she choked. 'Forgive me for appearing dense, but I'm afraid you're talking in riddles.'

'It is I who should beg forgiveness, my dear,' he replied gently. 'But with what small excuse I have for my behaviour, I can only tell you that meeting you has been the most electrifying experience of my life.'

'It—has?' she gasped faintly, her eyes wide again.

'It has,' he unhesitatingly confirmed. 'Leaving aside the lies and the deceit I've practised, it's the honest truth that no sooner did you and I meet than I began to feel more alive than at any time I can remember. Is it any wonder that I shouldn't want you to leave me, but should want you to stay?'

What he was saying was 'electrifying' her, but she was still trying hard to keep up with him when she offered a husky-sounding, 'I—er—made you feel alive?'

'From the very first,' he confirmed, and added, 'Forgive my bluntness, but not just sexually either.'

'Not?' she questioned, and began to feel more lost than ever when slowly he moved his head from side to side. Then suddenly her whole being started to become taut with restrained excitement. Because all at once, in those moments of tangled thoughts, one single thought had magically separated itself from the rest of the quagmire that was in her head!

That thought, that startling thought that, if it was not just sexual, this—whatever it was—then could it *incredibly* be . . . She couldn't finish the sentence. Didn't dare finish the sentence. She looked into the serious grey eyes of the proud man who held her hands—the proud man who must have hared after her to the airport. She gazed at the man who looked unflinchingly back, the proud man who had withstood her publicly serving him a vicious blow to his face and who even then had not told her to go to the devil, and suddenly her heart began to labour, erratically and painfully, within her. And Erith knew then that she would stay and listen, indeed had to stay and listen to every word Dom wanted to say, no matter how much of a let-down the outcome might be.

She was aware that he was silently waiting, watching—just as if he was giving her this moment of time to see something for herself. When his eyes stayed steady on hers, refusing to look away, refusing to let her look away, she took a long and deep breath, and then quietly, 'I think I sh-should—like you to—go on,' she said, a little shakily.

Dom delayed only a moment and raised both her hands to his lips and kissed them. Then, appearing a degree strained himself, even while he refused to look anywhere but into her eyes, he murmured, 'You delight me so much, do you not know that, Erith?'

'I . . .' she began helplessly.

'It has been so from the beginning,' he smiled.

'H-has it?'

He nodded, then had her clinging fast to his hands, as he told her, 'It seems incredible to me, now that the answer is so clear, that I should have taken so long to recognise why it is that I find such joy just being with you. Why, without knowing why, I should feel so alive just at being in your company!' He broke off, and seemed to need to take a steadying breath, before going on, oh, so tenderly, 'How could I, my dear, dear Erith, have fallen in love with you and yet not recognised it, do you suppose?' he asked.

'Y . . .' Her voice didn't make it. She swallowed on a knot of emotion, and suddenly started to tremble.

She realised that her trembling must have communicated itself to him, for he exclaimed abruptly, 'I've alarmed you!' and she was not sure that he did not lose some of his colour when, 'My feelings for you embarrass you! You do not wish me to be in love with you!' he exclaimed, with such anguish in his tone that Erith hurriedly found her voice.

'It's not that!' she told him quickly. 'It's just that . . .' She broke off, his words repeating and repeating in her brain, stunning her as they bounced back at her. 'You're—truly—in love with me?' she just had to question.

'Truly!' Dom wasted no time in telling her. And, as if believing that her needs had to be answered before his own, and with her hands safe in his firm hold, 'I knew within hours of your being at Jahara that there was something special about you,' he softly breathed.

'Back then?' Erith questioned.

'Back then,' he agreed gently, though he owned, 'I denied it, of course. And then one morning you arrived at breakfast, and I looked up and, incredibly, felt something stir in my heart just to see you. Is it any wonder that, having grown more and more enchanted by you, I should immediately decide to take the morning off?'

'You took me for a drive round Jahara,' Erith whispered, feeling winded still and needing time to take in what it was he was, so staggeringly, saying.

'And,' Dom took up, 'you said that you thought it beautiful.'

'You remember that?' she asked, her eyes fixed on his face.

'That memory was one of the few things I had on which to pin my hopes when everything suddenly started to look very bleak for me,' he replied.

'Bleak for you?' she questioned, and perhaps looked as confused as she felt, for suddenly Dom let go her hands and cupped her face.

'My dear Erith,' he murmured, looking gently into her face. 'Words, actions, are in a furore within me. I want to kiss your sweet lips, beg you to tell me how it is with you—can you bear to love me a little, I wonder? And yet—I've behaved so abominably to you, have lied, deceived and, when you've done nothing but be your dear self, I have barked and snarled at you. Can you wonder,' he asked, 'that I don't know quite where the hell I am, or what I should do first? Somehow, though, from the sawdust I seem to have for a brain at this moment, I have a conviction that you deserve, from the love and respect I feel for you, that I should first try to explain all that has been in me and that has made me act in the dishonest way I have.'

'You—love me?' Erith asked him quietly.

'I adore you,' he answered sincerely, and as her heart leapt she saw that, when she could as easily have told him that she did not want his love, the fact that she had asked the question she had was of some encouragement to him.

'You weren't barking and snarling the whole of the time,' she reminded him, a tremulous smile coming to her mouth.

Her smile faded when suddenly his head started to come nearer. She knew he was going to kiss her. But suddenly he checked, then pulled back. And Erith knew then, as his hands left her face, that it was as a point of honour with him that he felt he must not kiss her until he had apologised by explaining in full.

He looked at her for a second or two, then declared. 'This love that started to stir in me for you, Erith, has been most uncomfortable to live with.' And, by way of explanation for that remark, 'Until I met you,' he went on, 'I had never been so constantly affected by such extreme contrasts of mood.'

'I—made you—er—moody?' she questioned.

'I, and my conscience, were responsible for the swings of my mood,' he replied. 'You, and the way my heart would lift each time I saw you, made me unsure that I liked what you were able to do to me. You, and the way you only had to ask had I heard any news of your stepsister yet, were responsible for my abruptness with you at times.'

'Your—er—conscience started to trouble you?'

'Too often,' he smiled. 'It happened that day we drove round Jahara. In no time I'd swung from wanting very much to stay in your company, to deciding that I'd much better things to do in my study. Then, when the very next day, having purposely avoided you and sure I didn't give a damn about you anyway, you came to my study looking for me and—what did I know—just to turn and see you standing there—and my heart was suddenly singing.'

'Honestly?' Erith gasped, her eyes shining.

'Believe it,' Dom assured her, and, after looking into her lovely eyes for long moments, 'Can you wonder,' he asked, 'that, having deprived myself of your company all that time, I should decide that I wanted to know more about you? I then thought it was time I had a whole day off.'

'You told me you had to go to Cuzco,' Erith inserted, and received a warm look from him that it appeared that, not only were they totally on the same wavelength, but that there seemed little that she had forgotten either.

'But we went further than Cuzco. I took you to see the fortress of Sacsahuaman, and it was there that you suddenly looked at me with those large green eyes and, as my heartbeats started to quicken, I, for the first time ever, felt unexpectedly vulnerable. I thought it was time we got away from there, and fast.'

'I—er—think I felt something much the same a little later on that very day,' she found herself shyly confessing.

'You're not going to leave it there, I hope,' Dom hinted when it seemed she had said all she was going to say.

'We were having a picnic in that most wonderful spot near Pisac,' she went on, 'and suddenly I realised that I'd never been so aware of a man as I was aware of you.'

'You're being honest with me now?' he questioned tautly.

'Oh, yes,' she confirmed, and with even more truth confided, 'Although I confess that I denied to myself later that it had been so, that didn't stop me from feeling very confused about you—and a little nervous too.'

'You're not *afraid* of me?' he asked abruptly, clearly not liking that idea at all.

'If you remember,' she at once quietened any such notion, 'it was I who closed the door to this suite.'

'So you did,' he said, and seemed to relax visibly. 'I'll thank you for that later,' he promised, and resumed, 'But first you must forgive me that my next action, when I knew quite definitely that your stepsister and Filipo were living in the north, was to quite deliberately take you south.'

'Why did you?' she asked, but there was no anger in her this time that he had deliberately lied when he'd told her that he'd just taken a phone call to say that Filipo had been seen in Arequipa.

'You had just told me that you thought you might as well return home—and I knew, whatever else I didn't know, that I didn't want you to leave me.'

'Oh!' she sighed, loving every word he was saying, then she was remembering, 'You were like a bear with a sore head the next morning!'

'How else would I be?' he enquired gently. 'I've said that I've never lied the way I lied to you. I'd been awake all night nursing a troublesome conscience.'

'Oh, Dom,' she said softly, on the instant ready to forgive him everything, 'You didn't stay that short-tempered with me, though,' she stated quietly.

'How could I?' he replied tenderly. 'We had one marvellous day in Arequipa, a day when there were no thoughts for me but our two selves. In fact, by the time we were sitting down to dinner that night, I'd enjoyed my day with you so much I was not at all ready to allow outside influences to intrude. I,' he smiled, 'hadn't taken into my calculations that you would remind me by asking, "Were there any messages?".'

'I'm sorry,' Erith swiftly apologised. If she had ever been furious with him, that fury was far from her now.

'Don't be sorry!' he exclaimed as though it offended him to hear her apologise. 'You've much, so very much to forgive me for. I have lied to you, deliberately told you untruths,' he continued. 'Why, only the very next day I found I was lying for all I was worth, when I told you that I had confirmation that my nephew and his woman friend were touring.'

Erith was by then ready to forgive him everything. She thought her heart would never beat normally again. 'We flew to Juliaca that same morning,' she remembered.

'And that was where, standing on the *altiplano*, by the purple corn, that a feeling came over me of wanting to hold you, and keep on holding you. Later, in your hotel room when you were ill, and I did hold you in my arms, I knew just why. I, my beautiful Erith,' he uttered tenderly, 'realised that I was in love with you.'

'Then?' she asked, remembering how comforted she'd felt at being in his arms.

'Right then,' he assured her, and for a long while Erith just sat and looked at him and began to wonder how she could ever have accused him of just being solely interested in bedding her. How could she ever have forgotten the way he had tended her, the way he had sat with her and had looked after her when she had been ill?

Remembering that, though, she suddenly remembered something else, and 'Oh!' the small sound broke from her.

'What is it?' Dom questioned urgently, ready to slay every one of her dragons.

'I—er...' She didn't want him to think she was being critical, but, 'You said you'd send a cable to my father and stepmother, but I don't suppose you did.' She was about to add that it didn't really matter because Audra would be relieving their anxieties by soon arriving in Ash Barton in person. Dom, however, forestalled her.

'I may not have sent a cable on the day I said I would, but the message we agreed upon *was* sent,' he revealed.

'It was?' Her heart was full of love for him that he had indeed eased her family's anxieties. Audra, she knew, would quiet any concern they might feel that she wasn't with her, by passing on her message that she was taking a look at Peru, and would be home shortly. 'When did you send the cable?' she asked Dom, her eyes warm on his face. 'A day later?' she suggested softly.

For long moments he sat and just looked at her. Then, as if suddenly recalling she had asked a question, 'To be exact,' he replied, 'a week ago last Friday.'

'A week ago I...' Her voice faded in absolute astonishment. 'But I didn't give you their address until...' Again her voice faded when Dom all at once smiled.

'I already had the address. If you cast your mind back to that Friday, you may remember that that was the day you had your stolen bag returned.'

'The policeman was waiting for us when we returned from our drive around Jahara,' she recalled.

'And you checked your belongings.' Dom took up. 'Among which was a letter addressed to Mr and Mrs Hector Carter. When at lunch you said how worried your father and stepmother would be while they waited for news. I discovered I could recall their address.'

'You...' Erith was speechless.

'Made use of it to send a cable in your name stating that your stepsister was well and happy. It seemed the least I could do,' Dom volunteered.

Silently Erith looked at him, her love for him uppermost that, out of the sensitivity that was his, he had, so long ago, given peace of mind to her father and stepmother.

'Oh, Dom,' she breathed as the emotion she felt for him started to overflow, and quite unthinkingly, 'is it any wonder that I love you?' she asked—and only became aware of what she had disclosed when she saw the totally stunned look that came over his face.

Then her hands were in his hold, and he was gripping them as he demanded hoarsely, 'Do you? Is that the truth?' Erith's lips parted, but, having realised that she had revealed the truth of her feelings, she could only nod. 'Are you sure?' Dom insisted, his hands, whether he knew it or not, crushing hers.

'I'm positive,' she whispered softly.

'Since when?' He wanted more convincing, his fingers clenched hard over hers.

'Since yesterday—out on the lake,' she replied truthfully.

'When?' he demanded, his mind obviously busy. 'Before or after I half frightened you to death?'

'You didn't half frighten me to death,' she denied.

'I didn't?' He looked sceptical, and Erith knew he was remembering the startled way she had jerked away from him.

'I'd just then realised that I was in love with you,' she told him shyly, and owned, 'It—sort of—threw me.'

'My darling!' he breathed, and suddenly she was in his arms.

Gently he kissed her. Then, for long, long moments, he just held her close up to him, and as Erith's heart beat so loudly that she thought she could hear it, he kissed her long and tenderly again.

Then, whispering endearments in his own language as well as in English, Dom held her firmly against his heart for a long while before gently kissing her again, then pulling back to look adoringly into her face.

'It's true—I'm not dreaming?' he asked.

'Am I?' she questioned, and he kissed her again.

'I love you with all that's in me,' he stated quietly, and there was no mistaking the sincerity in his eyes. 'I've been in such hell over you, my sweet Erith,' he revealed. 'Deceiving when I've never deceived in my life, then finding I'm scared to utter another word in case, when

I've vowed to myself to be only ever truthful to you from now on, I should, before I've had a chance to try to explain, lie to you again.'

'When was this?' she asked, trusting him, not doubting him.

'Surely you noticed how this morning it seemed I could barely say a civil word to you?' he questioned.

'Because you were afraid you might have to lie again before you could clear everything up?' she questioned, and received a warm look for her understanding.

'That, and the fact that I've felt on a blade's edge about how you were going to react when I did get around to confessing everything,' he replied, then he told her, 'I started down this whole appalling path of deceit purely because I didn't want you to go away. When I realised exactly why it was that I didn't want you to go away—because I'd fallen in love with you—I dwelt in hell. It was then that I realised too that it was quite likely you would never so much as want to speak to me, much less stay with me, once you knew how I had tricked you.'

'Has it been such hell?' Erith questioned softly, and loved him when he first kissed her face, and when he gently laid his lips over hers.

'Torment is understating what I've been through,' Dom answered her question, and went on to qualify, 'There were some distinctly heavenly times too. Times when just to be with you, walking with you, not even talking or touching, made me feel so good inside you just wouldn't believe. At others—did you even like me? I asked myself again and again at Lake Titicaca, and then I knew more heaven when I kissed you—and was never more shaken when you responded the way that you did!'

'I was so dreadfully afraid I'd given myself away,' Erith confessed.

'And I was afraid to believe what my heart wanted to believe—that you must care, mustn't you? You'll never know the mass of contradictions I've been in my head.'

'I'd like to,' she hinted, and laughed lightly from pure happiness, and, when he seemed totally delighted with her, they kissed, again, and again.

'So,' Dom said, determinedly putting some space between them as he looked down into her all at once pink-tinged complexion, 'there was I, after coming off the lake, having to spend an entire afternoon worrying about you.'

'You were worried about me!'

'I thought I'd frightened you by seeming too amorous,' he replied openly. 'I came to your room to try to reassure you. Only you had little on but a bath towel, and then you started to annoy me, then went on to stir jealousy in me by telling me you'd been kissed before, I suddenly found I'd taken you in my arms—you,' he smiled, 'know the rest.'

'I—er—it wasn't that I was afraid of you that—made me run and bolt myself in the bathroom,' she thought she should tell him, and loved him the more when a broad grin spread across his features. She thought for a moment that he was going to make some comment on the way she had streaked, utterly naked, from him.

But if he was remembering such things he must have decided to save them for another time, for he did not allude to the way she had catapulted from the bed, but answered only, 'While you couldn't be aware of it, my sweet one, there was a certain reserve in your warm response of a woman who'd never been in—that situation before. I knew, just the same, that it wasn't me you were running from when the porter knocked at the door, but a natural modesty that made you dive to hide when you thought someone might—as I had—walk in at any second.'

Erith reached up and gently pressed her lips to his cheek. She'd no idea that there had been any trace of reserve in her response to him, but she was now ready, eager in fact, to believe every word he said. 'You'd—er—gone when I came out,' she murmured.

'I waited a few minutes,' Dom owned tenderly, one hand gently caressing the side of her face. 'Then suddenly it somehow hit me that it just wasn't right to take what you had seemed prepared to give, not while all my lies and deceit were between us.'

'Oh, Dom!' she whispered, the knowledge endorsed for her that he *was* an honourable man, and that it was not just lust for her body that motivated him.

'Sweet Erith!' he breathed, but, after long seconds of just gazing at her as if hardly able to believe that she was here close with him in the shelter of his arm, he went on, 'I got out of your room while I still could—and then spent more time in agony knowing that I couldn't go on like that. Things came to a head for me over dinner that night.'

'I remember you seemed to have a lot on your mind when I said goodnight,' Erith realised.

'Thanks to you,' he said wryly.

'Me—why?' she wanted to know, and was again warmed—and startled—by his reply.

'It was my dearest wish,' he began, 'to have you living with me at Jahara.'

'It was!' Erith echoed, in shaken exclamation.

'Oh, yes, my love,' he replied. 'Many times I've wanted to tell you everything—fear that you would at once leave kept me silent. But when, just then, everything started to look bleak for me, I thought of your response when I held you in my arms, and also the fact that you had thought Jahara beautiful. You *had* to have some small caring for me to have responded the way you had, I thought, and I just had to pin my hopes on the fact that you *might* love me a little, and *might*, unlike my mother who is also European, be prepared to live here. I decided,' he ended, 'to try and find out how you felt about living at Jahara during dinner that night.'

Erith's eyes were again large in her face as last night's topic of conversation at dinner came back to her. And suddenly her heart was drumming more wildly than ever it had before. Because, if she was remembering correctly—and she owned that she was feeling too strung up then to be sure—then hadn't Dom, when asking her views, put the question 'Do you think a woman should stay in her husband's country for love?'? Surely he couldn't mean... She was trembling again, trying desperately hard not to think such lovely thoughts. 'You—er—told me about your parents, and—how they'd split up,' she mentioned quietly.

'And you, instead of telling me what I wanted to hear, gave me a lecture on honesty that little short of crucified me,' he replied. Erith was still staring at him when he went on, 'You stated your opinion that honesty was the basis for any relationship—and gave me plenty to think about.'

Remembering her own tormented night of sleep, 'You didn't sleep well?' she asked.

'If at all,' he replied. 'Who could sleep with what I'd got on my conscience? It didn't take me long to realise that if I wanted to get anywhere with you then I was going to have to clear all grains of deception out of the way. I, my darling,' he said, placing a gentle kiss on her brow, 'wanted that honest basis for us.'

Erith smiled, a loving smile. She had been in some torment herself, but Dom, her dear Dom, had been in agony. 'Was that why you came to my room early this morning to tell me that Audra and Filipo weren't touring any more?'

'Correction, sweet love,' he said with an answering adoring smile, 'I'd vowed never to lie to you again—my precise words were "I know the exact location of your stepsister and Filipo".'

'So they were,' she laughed, was soundly kissed for her trouble, and was uncaring then that his uncommunicative countenance on the flight had been because he'd been afraid he might have to tell another lie before he'd had time to confess to the lengths of his deception.

'Which reminds me,' he resumed, again putting some small daylight between their two bodies, 'how I didn't seem able to keep my hands off you the last time I was in your bedroom...'

'Ah!' Erith exclaimed as something clicked in her brain. 'That was why you booked me into a suite.'

'I wanted to be private with you when I confessed everything—and I didn't want to be sidetracked,' Dom took up. 'In fairness to you, though, I felt I had to wait until we were here in Lima before I said anything. Then, if everything did go badly for me—and I was trying with all I had not to dwell on that—your stepsister would be but a three-quarters-of-an-hour flight away and...'

'And what would you have done?' Erith asked quietly.

Dom gave an expressive movement of his shoulders, then told her solemnly, 'I haven't been able to face looking at that possibility.' Gently then they kissed, and as he pulled back, 'That flight here from Juliaca was murder. But there was no way I was going to start our oh, so private discussion on an aircraft.'

'You said, when we arrived here, that there was something you wanted to say,' Erith gently reminded him.

'My timing was all wrong, wasn't it?' he said softly, recalling how a room maid had appeared in the corridor at just that moment. 'I took off to try and get myself together, to get some composure, to try and find a modicum of calm,' he enlightened her.

'It was as bad as that?' Erith crooned.

'You can have no idea,' he replied. 'It was while I was out that—with my stricken conscience again giving me hell—I decided to return to the hotel and to start making restitution by putting a call through to my nephew.'

'Oh, dear,' Erith smiled, realising at once what must have happened.

'"Oh, dear" is mild compared to the sweat I was in ten minutes after my call,' he grinned, and told her about his phone call to his nephew. 'I was midway into telling Filipo that if he was interested in having his job back then he'd better present himself and his lady friend in Lima straight away, when Filipo replied that while he would catch the very next plane, he and Audra had finished with each other. He then said how the day before he'd driven her to the airport to catch a plane to Lima.'

'You thought she might book into this hotel?'

Dom shook his head. 'It didn't even cross my mind as I asked Filipo if he thought she would fly straight on to England. "Who knows?" Filipo asked, then suggested that from what he knew of her it was quite likely that she'd take a look round Lima first to see "who was in town". I asked if she had money and he said that she was as hard pressed as him just then, but that he'd given her one or two expensive pieces of jewellery which she'd probably sell if she couldn't somehow get someone else to pay her hotel bill. I came off the phone,' Dom continued, 'realising that, even broke, Audra Billington would stay at only the best hotels. It was then,' he smiled, 'that I started to sweat. You were resting in your room, I thought, when I decided to ring reception to check if a Señorita Billington was registered.'

'They told you she was?' Erith questioned, quite riveted by all he was telling her.

'I waited, certain that I was panicking unnecessarily and that I'd only my guilty conscience to blame for that.

When reception confirmed my worst imaginings, by querying did I mean Señorita *Audra* Billington, I realised I had to get to you and confess everything before you and your stepsister met. I don't remember covering the distance from my door to yours,' he told her with a smile. 'But I was still hammering on your door trying to make you wake up and see me, when a porter came along and told me that he had seen the flame-haired lady leaving her apartment with a blonde lady. Fear was in my heart, my darling,' Dom admitted, 'when, hardly able to credit that my luck could be so against me that you had accidentally found your stepsister before I could explain anything, I questioned the porter. "They were without luggage, of course," I suggested. "But no, *señor*," he told me, "they had luggage, large luggage, both of them".'

'Oh, my darling!' Erith whispered. 'What did you do?'

Dom gave her a look of pure happiness for that 'darling', then he was saying, 'What would I do? I instantly found a cab and raced for the airport, terrified the whole time that you'd have already flown from me.'

'Terrified—you?' she questioned gently.

'Most definitely,' he replied. 'Although the taxi driver put his foot down, that journey seemed to go on for ever. But, when my mind was filled with so many agitated thoughts, it was on that nightmare journey that one particular piece of knowledge surfaced and, the closer I got to the airport, became sound and unerring knowledge.'

'What piece of knowledge was that?' she asked softly, and was gently kissed before Dom answered.

'I love you, with everything that's in me, my dear heart. It seems to me now that there was never a time when it wasn't so.' And, as Erith snuggled closer to him, 'Which perhaps explains why, within hours of knowing you, I took you to Jahara. I was later to remember that you thought Jahara beautiful, later as I became slightly demented and wondered how all this—my deceiving you—would all end that; wanting to marry you above all else, but...'

'Marry!' Erith jerked upright in his arms, to stare at him, her heartbeats wild again.

'Of course, marry,' he answered proudly. It was very clear from the very look of him that never once had he ever considered, let alone thought of, asking her to be his mistress.

'I see,' Erith murmured, and relaxed back in his arms, deciding that she would confess her previous thoughts some other time, for now what Dom was saying was far more interesting. 'You—er—wanted to marry me, but...' she prompted softly.

'But I had to think seriously of our future happiness. You're so dear to me, my Erith,' he murmured, 'and, unlike my mother, you had seemed quite enchanted with my home. But, should I be so fortunate that you were not only still speaking to me when I confessed my sins, but did agree to marry me, what if, living permanently in Jahara, you should awake one morning and not find it beautiful at all?'

'Oh, my dear!' Erith whispered, remembering how—was it only yesterday—she had thought him to be brooding about something. Suddenly then, though, she began to feel alarmed and, albeit hesitantly, just had to ask, 'But you—er—decided to—er—risk it?' she questioned, as stress threw her into confusion, hoping with all her heart that he had decided in favour of asking her to marry him, because she just didn't know how she was going to face it if this time of being in his arms was all there was—and he was sending her away.

Her heart was once more turning cartwheels when, looking deeply into her eyes, Dom told her softly, 'You're part of me now, my love. Though it was during that nightmare taxi ride to the airport when, with so much going on in my head, I recalled how I'd once told you "For you, anything", and it was then, as I thought, for Erith, if I can get to her in time, *everything*, that I suddenly knew that if you didn't like Jahara it didn't matter. Because the one fact that leapt out at me then was that, where my father before me had refused to leave Peru for his love, while I might return periodically to Jahara, I could only live where you live.'

'*Dom!*' Erith cried, startled. 'You—m-mean you'd— leave Jahara—*for me*?'

'Of course,' he replied unequivocally.

'Y-you love me that much?' she whispered, her voice barely audible—Jahara meant the world to him, she knew it did!

'Oh, yes,' he said quietly, sincerely, and asked, a touch of strain coming to his tone, just as if he still wasn't sure, 'Are you going to allow me to spend the rest of my life showing you how very much I mean that?'

'Y-you're asking me to m-marry you?'

His expression was taut, unsmiling, and he looked as though he was under a good deal of strain. 'Will you?' he clipped.

Erith was still trying to recover from her incredulity that he was prepared to live away from Jahara for her, and as love for him swelled up in her she knew just then why it was that she had let Audra have her air-fare with so little argument. Despite not knowing anything of what he'd told her, she loved Dom so much she just didn't want to leave.

She swallowed hard on emotion, and confessed, 'I can clearly remember waking at Jahara and feeling content, and glad to be there,' and as Dom continued to stare severely at her as tensely he waited for her answer, 'Jahara already feels like home to me,' she smiled, and added, 'and I should like very much to live there, please.'

His head came nearer, but just before he kissed her, 'In plain English,' he demanded, 'is that a "yes" to my proposal?'

'*Si,*' she laughed joyously, and was kissed, and once more kissed, and then, as Dom drew back and gazed with burning grey eyes at her green eyes and pinkened skin, 'Oh, yes, yes, yes, my love!' she whispered.

* * * * *

*Watch out for Bliss's story
next month in
FLIGHT OF DISCOVERY*

my VALENTINE 1992

Celebrate the most romantic day of the year with
MY VALENTINE 1992—a sexy new collection of four
romantic stories written by our famous Temptation
authors:

GINA WILKENS
KRISTINE ROLOFSON
JOANN ROSS
VICKI LEWIS THOMPSON

My Valentine 1992—an exquisite escape into a romantic
and sensuous world.

 Harlequin Books®

HARLEQUIN Temptation

Rebels & Rogues

All men are not created equal. Some are rough around the edges. Tough-minded but tenderhearted. Incredibly sexy. The tempting fulfillment of every woman's fantasy.

When it's time to fight for what they believe in, to win that special woman, our Rebels and Rogues are heroes at heart.

Josh: He swore never to play the hero . . . unless the price was right.

THE PRIVATE EYE by Jayne Ann Krentz. Temptation #377, January 1992.

Matt: A hard man to forget . . . and an even harder man not to love.

THE HOOD by Carin Rafferty. Temptation #381, February 1992.

At Temptation, 1992 is the Year of Rebels and Rogues. Look for twelve exciting stories about bold and courageous men, one each month. Don't miss upcoming books from your favorite authors, including Candace Schuler, JoAnn Ross and Janice Kaiser.

Available wherever Harlequin books are sold. RR-1

HARLEQUIN
PROUDLY PRESENTS
A DAZZLING NEW CONCEPT IN ROMANCE FICTION

One small town—twelve terrific love stories

Welcome to Tyler, Wisconsin—a town full of people you'll enjoy getting to know, memorable friends and unforgettable lovers, and a long-buried secret that lurks beneath its serene surface....

JOIN US FOR A YEAR IN THE LIFE OF TYLER

Each book set in Tyler is a self-contained love story; together, the twelve novels stitch the fabric of a community.

LOSE YOUR HEART TO TYLER!

The excitement begins in March 1992, with WHIRLWIND, by Nancy Martin. When lively, brash Liza Baron arrives home unexpectedly, she moves into the old family lodge, where the silent and mysterious Cliff Forrester has been living in seclusion for years....

WATCH FOR ALL TWELVE BOOKS OF THE TYLER SERIES
Available wherever Harlequin books are sold

TYLER-G